FINDING SCARLET

KIRSTEN PURSELL

To new beginnings...

Table of Contents

ONE

I KNOW why Nicholas Sparks sets all his books in North Carolina. It is beautiful, romantic, and full of hope—maybe false hope, but hope. That's exactly why I chose South Carolina instead. It was equally beautiful, but it did not evoke the same sense of romanticism that I associated with North Carolina. It did not set me up with unrealistic expectations like North Carolina did.

Yes, I chose South Carolina because Nicholas Sparks ruined North Carolina for me. Although not all his books ended with a happily ever after. Mostly, they ended in tears for me. Love stories with sad endings. Or happy endings from sad beginnings. But I couldn't escape the beauty of the coast he described.

After years of reading his books as a sort of guilty pleasure, I had developed an image in my mind of a perfect place to live. Endless beaches and majestic sunrises and sunsets. When it came time for me to choose where to begin anew, in my fifties, it was the first place I considered. However, I was imperfect and did not want to start over with expectations too high. That's how I rationalized it. I did not have the same expectations of South Carolina. I could have my own story there without any shadows being cast by another Nicholas Sparks novel.

When asked why I would leave the comfort of my life on the West Coast, I tell people that divorce drove me away; I wanted and needed a place to begin anew. It's a half-truth.

I was dying to leave my Southern California home most of my life. People spend their entire lives in one place, and I never wanted to be that person. I often felt like I was suffocating in one spot, knowing a world of experiences was just around the corner. Or maybe I was just anxious, knowing there was so much to see and do outside of my life's bubble.

Most people consider Oceanside a perfect place to live. It morphed from a military seaside community to one of the largest suburbs of San Diego. My dad's military service first brought my parents here. They fell in love with the proximity to the ocean and the affordable home prices. It was idyllic, and over time, it began to outgrow its military town label and become an actual tourist destination.

I was a lifeguard at the city beaches in the summer during high school and college. Back then, the beaches were covered in white sand. Erosion has given way to rocks, less oceanfront land, and the annual dredging project, an effort to add back sand. Oceanside's pier boasts being the longest wooden pier on the West Coast.

I had a front-row seat as Oceanside grew into a tourist destination over the years. But I often felt like an outsider looking in, trying to find my place there.

The fact I raised my family in a place I never felt part of brings me no sadness. Their experiences growing up were so much less dramatic than mine. Of course, that's perceived drama. Self-inflicted mostly. I never felt like I personified the California girl people saw me as. I was insecure. Never felt pretty enough. Never quite embodying the stereotype I drank like Kool-Aid: blonde, skinny, perfect figure in an itty-bitty bikini, ditsy, carefree, sun-loving. The idealized girl from movies and magazines. I knew no one like that. I knew that then. But even so, my home never quite felt like a place I belonged.

My decades-long marriage is over. My children were raised and live life mostly on their terms. I embrace that before I become too old or bitter or resentful for a life not fully lived, it's time to try the unfamiliar parts. I want green and the ocean. I want history at my doorstep. I want weekend trips to Europe.

On my own. Divorced. God, that's such a strong word. I would say it was mutually earned, but, in the end, I deserve more credit for the demise of my marriage than he ever did, acknowledging that no marriage solely ends at the hand of one person. Both are complicit. Maybe we share credit. But the blame is on me.

TWO

WE SIGNED ON THE LINES. Shane's signature across from mine, perfectly spaced apart. Our initials mixed throughout the mediation document, almost as if we were buying a house. We were signing a document together for the last time. This time, it was untying us, telling the courts that we had cordially agreed to dissolve our marriage through mediation. It wasn't perfect. He was bitter. I knew that. But we got through it. As a final act of our ability to coexist, we agreed on how to end our marriage and move forward.

The mediator, a stoic woman in her sixties with unbridled calm, commended us on how well we treated each other throughout the process. She didn't see all the email exchanges. She didn't need to. We got to the finish line without any real carnage, a few hurt feelings perhaps, and a bruised ego. All we had to do now was wait six months, and we would officially no longer be connected by marriage. I thought I'd feel relief. I thought the weight would be lifted. Instead, the pain that radiated within me at having failed my marriage worsened before

4

dissipating into a sense of calm and satisfaction at having had the courage to put myself first.

He hugged me as we left the mediator's office to go our separate ways.

"How'd we get here?" he asked, holding me close in a final, awkward embrace.

"You couldn't forgive me." I reminded him.

"I forgave you a long time ago."

"But you would have doubted me forever. And that would be worse than not forgiving me."

Yes, the constant shadow that I might lose my way again would always be near in those moments when things got tenuous, and they would because marriage is not perfect. Ever. But less so when one of you wronged and it would never feel totally right again.

The story is as old as time. A spouse is unfaithful. Ours was no different. My friends, the ones who don't really know me, assumed I was the woman scorned. They believed that it was only possible to seek divorce if the husband was unfaithful. They would offer unsolicited assessments of Shane when they thought my guard was down. I could only suggest to them that what was on the surface was not necessarily what the reality was. They would offer an embrace with a look of pity that I was being too kind to him; no man who hurts a woman should walk scot-free. My parting words as those superficial embraces released, "Maybe it wasn't him," left their mouths agape. Shane would have stayed, I know. But I could not.

AS FAR AS amicable divorce goes, it must have ranked as one of the nicest ever. No mudslinging. And he could have. No name-calling. Could have done that too. That sometimes made it worse. I kept waiting for the shoe to drop, for him to sling nasty slurs my way in hopes that by verbally retaliating, he might hurt me. But he did not. Then I wondered if maybe he'd wanted out all along and was just waiting for me to slip up so he could escape. It was an endless game that my mind played on me. One did not read or hear much about amicable divorces. I knew it was possible. And somehow, we had become the poster couple for harmonious uncoupling.

Financially, I knew I would be okay with minimal spousal support. I didn't realize until the divorce proceedings that the small inheritance I received from my parents' passing would not have to be shared. Conversely, he would not have to share his rather large one from his parents. Fortunately, we never needed to use what we'd each inherited, that money put away in anticipation of the day we could play with it in retirement. Aside from buying a home when the market was down, earmarking our inheritances was easily our most significant, if not only, financial success. We never touched it, even when we were tempted. I was grateful for that padding moving forward. I know it could have been much different. I saw acquaintances who weren't as fortunate in that regard.

As for everything else, we split equally. The retirement accounts, when looked at as a whole, offered a glimpse of a comfortable retirement. The picture looked significantly less liberating when each of us only got half. There wasn't much in our regular savings to split. To a degree, I suppose, we lived paycheck to paycheck. Raising a family in California on one income afforded financial challenges that made saving a formidable foe at times. I did odd job freelance work as opportunities presented themselves. However, we did not want for anything. Our kids, by all accounts, never needed anything. We took vacations. We lived like many of our Southern California contemporaries: at or above a reasonable means, but we made it work. Shane and I recognized that the kids were our priority, which was likely the first step in losing who we were as a couple. We thought we could always come back to that. Instead, we seemed to find refuge in being busy, avoiding the glaring reality that we were slipping farther away from each other even in the moments when we could have reconnected. That often seemed easier than the effort it would have taken to find common ground outside of our day-to-day lives.

We sold the house. Neither of us could realistically afford to buy the other out. Of all the things that nearly broke me, that was it. We raised our two children there. Had a lifetime of memories as a family there. But the kids were long gone, living life on their terms. They did not need a home base anymore. I knew, too, that selling my modest home in California meant getting enough cash to purchase something small in one of the Carolinas. It meant I could live on spousal support doing my freelance work, making a small income from graphic design projects and writing articles for several local publications. I needed to be creative. And at fifty-five years old, I wasn't about to bury myself in trying to convince the corporate world that an old woman, by their standards, not mine, could still bring value and creative energy to their place of business.

There were more questions for me than answers after the divorce was finalized, the house sold, assets divided, and my future a blank slate in front of me.

I PACKED the pieces of my life into assorted boxes. Some with purpose, others without. The moving truck came. And left. The parts of my life left behind fit neatly in the back of my gently worn but beloved BMW X3. Another excess we afforded ourselves when we probably should have bought an equally functional, much more affordable car. It was a symbol, I suppose. Shane had a high-profile position as Oceanside's city manager, and we would not skimp on appearances. Like so much in our marriage, I think to myself in hindsight.

I wanted Zero, our giant Baja rescue of unknown breeds, to come with me, but the pain on Shane's face said, "You owe me this much." It would have been selfish of me to insist on that. I cried for hours when Shane took him from me for the last time, when we said our last goodbyes without ever really saying the words.

In the weeks before moving away, I carefully mapped out my cross-country trek. I loaded the last of my things, closed the trunk, and was suddenly overcome by a wave of emotion. I had been fooling myself into thinking I was handling the feelings of it all with such ease. I was overcome, recognizing I was leaving all I'd known for decades to head out on some adventure that made no promises I'd be happier there than here.

I squelched the urge to panic at the thought that I might not be the person I thought I was after all. *What if I do not become who I think I can be in the face of that divorce? What if I am dull, empty, judged, remorseful, and worse yet, what if I become bitter?*

I shake it off, knowing I will find a way to be okay; I did the hard part. If I mess up trying to figure out who I want to be moving forward, I have proven I am resilient. I wasn't sad. I wasn't broken. I was just missing pieces. Moving forward would be full of unanswered questions. I would spend the rest of my life figuring that out.

At fifty-five.

I stood alone on the doorstep with a huge chapter of my life behind the door I'd just let fall closed behind me. I walked forward, confident I had made the right decision. I needed to be allowed to be me. I needed change. I proved that when the temptation of Carter Edmonds could not be resisted.

THREE

I WAS eager to start over but found myself abiding by the speed limit signs before me. As I deliberately made my way across the United States, I would cherish this time to process. I'm not sure I had done that in the chaos of emotions that defined the months leading up to and during my divorce. I was utterly alone with my thoughts on this highway to my future. I replayed the parts of the last year in my head. There was my divorce from Shane. And there were painful reminders of Carter. What he was. What he might have been. And, in the end, what he was not.

I knew I could be fine in the wake of my divorce. I knew, despite my emotional infidelity, that Shane and I had made a valid attempt to salvage our marriage. There were so many moments leading up to the end. There were days it felt real; others, like I had imagined the whole thing, not sure whether I had done what I did. In that sort of purgatory, while waiting for all hell to break loose, not an hour passed without me wondering if it even happened.

When Shane learned about Carter, I felt like I had been punched in the gut. At that moment, I realized that what I did wasn't just about me. I had been so caught up in feeling seen, in being wanted, that I closed off the fact I would crush Shane in the process. I was blinded by hope. And desire. I was selfish in those moments, looking to satisfy the empty parts of me. I did not think how this might hurt Shane, even if he knew, too, that our marriage was a thin twine of string ready to snap with the weight of uncertainty.

The almost of Carter was both a beautiful reminder that I could still feel like a woman and simultaneously a painful dose of reality that temptation is weighted differently. I felt Carter pull the strings. I was a marionette, willingly moving in the direction he pulled me. Ultimately, he called the shots. And I would be left a crumpled mess discarded on the floor when he was done playing with me. He wouldn't see it that way. But I knew better.

I did not sleep with Carter. But I was emotionally gone. I imagined him nonstop. I texted with him constantly. I shared my life. My intimate secrets and, above all, desires. He asked things of me, and I eagerly gave them. He, in return, made me feel beautiful. Ultimately, he quit before the stakes were irreparable for him. But the pieces of my life that had been fraying were suddenly ripped open in the aftermath of Carter. A marriage precariously close to the edge fell to the sea with the simple admission that I had reconnected with someone from my past.

"Yes or no?" Shane asked.

"What?"

"Do you want the extra plate?" He said, pointing to the two appetizer plates next to him as we

sat across from each other at one of our favorite downtown beachside breweries. He was annoyed.

"Where are you, Scar?"

"I'm here."

"Physically, yes. But you're off in another world. Kind of like you've been a lot lately."

"A lot? Really?"

"You haven't been yourself. That's all."

I wanted to hold it in. It wasn't the right place. But I felt like a ticking time bomb. Any second, I might explode if I kept it inside any longer.

"I reconnected with someone from my past."

"That's cool..." The gravity of the statement became evident as he stopped midsentence. Processing, he said, "Like an old girlfriend or an old boyfriend...Or, what?"

"Like somebody who meant a lot to me once."

And when he pressed how much we had reconnected, I was honest. "We didn't sleep together, but I would have." I suppose I didn't need to be that forthright. But it would have haunted me knowing I only gave an emotional half-truth.

The pain in Shane's face was unmistakable. He took a bite of the Brussel sprouts smothered in balsamic and sprinkled with blue cheese crumbles. He watched me as he ate, slowly chewing his food, digesting. I could tell he was thinking. Wondering how to address me considering my admission. He took a slow drink of his IPA and put it down. Then he spoke in his usual calm, steady, monotone voice.

"I look at you, and part of me sees this beautiful woman. And the other part of me wants to hate you for doing that." The beautiful part pained me. How many times over the years had I longed for him to call me that? He did not dispense with compliments easily, least of all with me.

"I didn't mean for it to happen. I didn't plan it," I said matter of fact.

"No one ever plans it. It's what they all say," he said softly under his breath while taking another sip of his beer as if to drown out his words.

"I heard that. I didn't look for it despite what you think. I was lonely. And you weren't willing to give me what I needed. Anything, really, when I felt the most lost and lonely in our marriage." He shook his head in plausible deniability.

"Was I supposed to just read your mind?"

I wanted to scoff. At that moment, it was a sobering reminder of why the trajectory of our marriage was headed for failure.

"No, because I told you what I needed. And you laughed it off like wanting that after so many years was an unrealistic request. You didn't want to be that man."

He thought about it. "I couldn't be that man, Scar. And I think you were okay with getting caught."

He was right. It was my out. But it was not my intention to hurt him, crush his soul. I knew he'd probably hate me. That didn't sink in until after he learned about it.

———

I WANTED to take my time as I traversed the United States. I had been driving for five hours before making my first stop in Las Vegas. I knew Las Vegas wasn't the straightest or fastest route to South Carolina. And even though it was not my favorite city, there was still something familiar, maybe even comforting, to me. While I could not understand the allure of spending money on extravagant excesses that Vegas demanded, it was where we came when Henry and Emily, our twins, had sports tournaments. The happiness of Vegas was remembering adventures with them.

There is nothing that makes me smile more than my children. They will always be my children, even though they are adults, twenty-five, and living very different lives. Neither of them acted surprised when I told them we were getting divorced. They had been out of the house for years. First college. Then, starting their careers. Henry was in his final year of law school in Michigan. Emily was trying to figure out her place in the world three years post-graduation. She was my free spirit. She found a way to make ends meet, never asking for help, always searching for the next great thing. She and Henry were complete opposites. Henry worked hard in everything. Emily was naturally talented, especially as an athlete. Sports events in Vegas usually meant Henry played on the B team while Emily played on the elite team, whether it was soccer, lacrosse, or volleyball. I tried to encourage Henry to do other things, but, in hindsight, I think he enjoyed not having to be in the limelight. He wanted Emily to have her moments to shine. They were night and day but were each other's biggest fans. It was a nice balance to have with twins.

Where Emily excelled athletically, Henry achieved academically. He didn't need sports to help him get into college. He applied to eight universities and was accepted to all, picking Stanford in the end. Emily had received a partial scholarship to play soccer at Arizona State University. Playing soccer lasted a year. She hated the routine. She came to us knowing we might be disappointed, "I just want to party and play and find myself." Shane was less than happy about that. Later that night, I would remind him about our separate college experiences, which included partying, playing, and finding ourselves. He did not like the reminder. It took Emily an extra year to graduate, but she did. She's still trying to find herself. Oddly, I thought how much our lives were currently running in parallel.

I exited the freeway, made a few right turns, and found myself driving into the familiar Hampton Inn on the outskirts of Vegas. It was a quick stop off the freeway. Safe. Unassuming.

I pulled into a spot that looked towards the front entrance and was well lit. Shane had always ensured we parked the cars where predators might ponder twice before striking. It made me smile, realizing that I, too, had adopted that way of thinking. A car full of my belongings, the parts and pieces I could fit in my vehicle, some I would take in with me, others I would chance to fate. I was confident the parking gods were in my favor.

As I walked into the hotel foyer, it felt surreal. There was no Emily dragging her tired feet behind me, no Henry with his head in his phone playing his games, no Shane bringing up the rear with our belongings. There was a disconnect without them there, unchartered territory for me. It felt like I was in a haze, half dreaming, half living.

Most days, I recognize that those moments of haze are temporary. I know that the road in front of me will give me clarity. But there are those moments that tell me I still get lost sometimes. They serve as just another reminder that it can still feel so unreal.

In those instances, I find myself thinking about the days after Shane first learned of my infidelity. I half expected him to tell me to pack my bags and leave. I would have stood my ground and said the house is half mine. I didn't know where I'd go. I had no plan. Ultimately, he did not tell me to leave, and we coexisted in the house, living like roommates, not the lifelong partners we had been.

I moved to the guest room that doubled as my office, the place where I would find sanctuary, where I painted, drew, or wrote. It was my creative space. In those days, I came to recognize that it wasn't any different than it had been. The only difference was that we didn't share a bed— a bed that felt empty even when we were together.

I walk to the check-in counter and pull out my phone. I am met with a memory popping up on my screen. It is of Zero. My heart sank. He looked so happy in his goofy ways.

I get my key, take the elevator to the fourth floor, and promptly plunk myself onto the bed. I pull open the memory of Zero. He was there the last days that Shane and I were married. If a dog could be a rock, he was that.

———

DAYS after I asked for the divorce, Shane and I walked side by side with Zero in tow, talking like that moment had been swallowed up by a big black hole. It was a surreal moment. It played games with my mind. I wondered how he could act so ambivalent. How do you find out your wife of thirty years had an emotional affair with another man and then act like you never learned the truth, like you didn't believe it happened? I thought my stomach would be less in knots in the post-admission days, but it continued to feel like a tightly wound ball of rubber bands. When he finally brought it up, I could feel the release as the bands began to snap in my belly. It stung, but the tension was lessening.

I thought the sense of relief would be immediate. The tension that had been building during the time I strayed to when he found out had been intense. I needed, no wanted, him to know what I had done. It was a test on all fronts. The potential repercussions life altering. But I told myself that's why we have affairs anyway.

We spent the last week living like it didn't happen. It had me questioning if it ever did. Maybe I didn't have an affair. Maybe an emotional affair isn't really an affair after all. And it might be easier to forgive. Perhaps it was just a figment of my imagination. Maybe if I tried hard enough, I could make the memory disappear. And maybe Shane would forgive me.

"It would have been easier if you just had a one-night stand." He was stoic and deliberate when he finally talked to me about it.

"I didn't sleep with him."

"You said that. But it's worse because you gave him parts of yourself."

"Because parts of me were so empty."

"And you sought him out." It was not a question; instead, an accusation.

"No. I didn't." The allegation annoyed me. I thought about how to say the next part. "Maybe when two people are both feeling empty inside, and they reach out at their most empty moments, they find a way to feel less empty together. Even just emotionally."

Zero yanked me forward, almost as if on cue. "Shit. That dog is going to dislocate my shoulder one of these days."

Shane didn't respond. I could tell he was off somewhere in the distance. This was the extent of the conversation we would have. I knew better than to be disappointed. It was how Shane's emotional cortex worked. Beyond that brief conversation, he won't talk about what happened or the fact I couldn't deny it when he said I would be happier if we were divorced. The fact that Shane suggested a one-night stand would have hurt less told me he understood the magnitude of the emotional void in our marriage.

I wasn't sorry. I didn't feel guilty. I did not regret the affair. I was crushed to the core when it ended. I was disappointed that I did not get to be touched by another man in the way that Carter had said he wanted to touch me. My body did not ache for touch. Shane still touched me. It ached to be desired, needed, and wanted beyond fulfilling a basic human need.

MY PHONE PINGED, startling me back to reality. It was Emily checking in to make sure I had made it safely to Las Vegas. I was the mom, but she mothered me sometimes, especially since the divorce. While generally shunning societal conventions, Emily was a traditionalist about family. She was staunchly supportive and defensive of all of us, especially Henry. She loved deeply with an innate ability to sense when things were falling off course. The beauty of divorcing later in life is the reality that your children have already forged their own identities and, in turn, relationships with each parent. Both Emily and Henry had relationships with me and Shane that were not tied together. While it may not have made the reality of divorce any less painful, it did make navigating their relationships with us easier.

I assured her I was fine with a series of emojis, to which she replied, "We really need to work on your emoji skills. Maybe a gif now and then?"

"Gifs are work. Even I know that."

"Haha."

"I love you, Emily."

"I love you, Mom,"

I laid the phone by my side on the bed and stared at the ceiling, allowing my eyes to rest.

I AM *wide awake at three thirty in the morning. My mind didn't get the memo to sleep another few hours or at least until the day's light begins seeping through the blinds that I never fully close. I turn to see him sleeping next to me. But not really. The space between us is a metaphorical one for the state of my marriage. It is over. Yet we still share the bed.*

When the holidays are over, and the kids' former bedrooms resume as office and an extra bedroom, we will figure out the next steps. Until then, I am tense about knowing he knows it is over. And I am angered that he does not seem to care. I grab my phone and send myself an email of prose that strikes in the darkness. The repressed poet in me always seems to find the most inopportune time for inspiration.

The space between us
I turn to see you on the other side of the bed
Within arm's reach
But miles between us
I touch you, but you are cold
Your heart beats, but not for me
The love we lost standing in front of us
One foot out the door
Waiting to run
Waiting for me to shoot the gun
Dodging bullets
Breaking glass
Hail of fire
Burning what?
It's not desire.
I desired another. Desperately. Deeply. I got caught. Or confessed. It is not always clear anymore how it played out.

THE EARLY MORNING sun peeks through the sides of the hotel blinds. I had somehow managed to find my way underneath the covers wearing the clothes I fell asleep in. Teeth were not brushed the night before. Bags untouched. I wondered how I managed not to pee all night. Yet, I felt refreshed.

I remembered that first morning I woke up alone in the bed I shared with Shane for thirty years. It was sobering. It was different than those mornings when one of us was out of town and the bed empty, either in a hotel, a friend's home, or our bed. I never felt empty then or like a part of me was missing. Shane had become a part of me.

For thirty years, he was the other half of the bed...even when he wasn't there. Even when we were separated, I could still feel his presence. But now, officially divorced, the reality that his space was no longer that was sobering.

I stretched my arms out wide, took a deep breath, and relished being alone in a hotel room for the first time as a single woman. It felt different. It was unfamiliar. But it was also a reminder that I had done it, that I had chosen my happiness over complacency.

FOUR

MY DRIVE east blurred as I drove from one city to the next, from one state to another. My mind wandered as I could no longer distinguish the spaces on the dashes dividing lanes. I replayed how I ended up on this God-forsaken road somewhere in the middle of nowhere on the road to my new life.

Shane. Discontent. Loneliness. The message from Carter. The back and forth. Seeing each other again. That was where we were tripped up. What little hope I had that I could hang on to my marriage and find ways to be content in the face of discontent came to an abrupt stop when Carter and I began down that road.

Carter Edmunds had been one of my many high school crushes. I didn't have a type. Carter was dorky and gangly. He was smart but also an amazing athlete. He didn't fit into any one mold. He was not a typical jock, even though he was tall and had great hair when he bothered to comb it. He wasn't a total nerd, either. He wore braces until the start of senior year. When those came off, it was glaringly apparent how handsome he was, his smile melting all of us. He gained confidence, maybe even bordering on arrogance that year. He knew girls loved him. He dated Darla Hines during our senior year, and he was loyal to her, which was another thing that made him sit on a pedestal high above everyone else. We had English and History together. I stared at him from the back of the class. Occasionally, he'd catch me staring at him, making me turn red in embarrassment as I tried to disguise what I had been doing.

We graduated from high school, having never said more than a passing hello to each other. We both went off to college. We ran into each other on rare occasions during summers in college when we would be home for break. He had morphed into a handsome man. I had also gained confidence during college, found flirting fun, and practiced on Carter. I gave him a hard time about holding back the goods from us while we were in high school.

"It's too bad only Darla got to experience you in high school," I told him one night in my early twenties before I met Shane.

"You were out of my league, Scar. I always had a crush on you."

"Awww. That's so sweet," I remember telling him. I had one too many drinks at that point. I leaned in and gave him a kiss. He did not kiss me back. He turned a bright shade of red and just looked down at his drink.

"What? You didn't like that?" I asked playfully.

He studied me hard at that moment. "No. I liked it a lot. I just don't want to kiss you when you've been drinking, is all."

"So now you're just a prude?"

"No. I just respect you too much."

"Oh." Well, that shut me up right then. "Okay. But you're never going to get another chance, Carter Edmunds." I remember getting so close to his face that I could feel him breathing, hoping, chancing he might kiss back anyway. But he did not. So I whispered in his ear, "You only ever get one shot with me." I paused. "And that was yours." I walked straight out of that bar.

That was the last time I saw Carter. I graduated from UCLA and moved back to the area to start my career. It wasn't what I thought I'd be doing, but the opportunity knocked to help set up the local museum of art, so I did. I would meet Shane at a city function years later. On the other hand, Carter played football in Washington and stayed there. This much I knew.

The fact that Carter reached out to me nearly forty years after we graduated took me by surprise. It was a simple friend request he sent on Facebook. Then there was a quick message: *Hey Scarlet, I hope you remember me and are well. After way too much time in Seattle, we've had enough of the gloomy, wet weather. Moving back to So Cal. Saw you're still in the old hood. Looking for options if you know of any.*

I had not thought about Carter since our encounter at the bar in college. Like many boys I had a crush on but never hooked up with, he faded away to the occasional thought. He did not attend high school reunions. I only went because I lived in the area and could supply tickets to the art museum for raffles. While I had left the art museum when the twins were still young, I was tied to it over the years. It was a source of pride for me, knowing I helped create something to support the arts in my community.

Of course, I accepted Carter's friend request and promptly stalked his page. I was impressed that he posted things about his life. He looked good. He had a little less hair than when we were in high school, but he maintained his fitness. His wife was pretty and clearly much younger. His two kids were in middle school. He looked like he had been living an ideal life.

I admittedly felt flattered that Carter had remembered me at all. I never thought myself memorable in those years. Unfortunately, I was forced to wait until college and beyond to blossom. I was a swimmer. My hair was constantly wet upon arriving at school and had a mind of its own. I mostly kept it in a ponytail or high on my head. I didn't have time to put on makeup after morning practice. On the rare day I wore makeup, I felt like everyone was staring at me, knowing full well that I didn't have a clue how to put it on. My clothes were simple: jeans or shorts and T-shirts with a sweatshirt. I liked being comfortable. I stayed in my lane and under the radar.

Hey Carter, good to hear from you. Sadly, or not, still here. Well, left and came back. It has changed. Lots of options in the area. Mostly good. I'll send realtor information.

I kept it simple. I sent him contact information for two realtors I knew. Realtors were ubiquitous and cutthroat. They were all too eager for the business. I wanted to avoid playing favorites. He could choose which one to work with.

Our text tone was casual at first. We dove into our lives in bits and pieces. Carter shared his story. He joined the Navy after college and served ten years as an officer, spending much of it overseas. When he returned, he was stationed back in Washington. He met his wife there. A second marriage, he admitted.

"Did you know Darla and I were briefly married?" he asked.

"I did. Sorry it didn't work out," I replied.

"Ha. I'm not. Learned a good lesson there." Laugh emoji.

Darla had been married at least three more times since Carter. She looked nothing like herself anymore. Too many injections in every part of her face left her looking awkward. Plastic surgeries did not make her more beautiful. She was on the eternal search to remain young but had become the poster child for too much of a good thing.

"She looks nothing like she used to," I said.

"Nope. But you do." I did not expect that.

"Ugh. I'm not sure that's a good thing." I admitted.

"You're kidding, right? I told you I had a crush on you." I felt flush remembering the night at the bar when I kissed him. "Remember?"

"Barely. And also a little embarrassed since I'm sure the alcohol made me feel empowered." He sent a laughing emoji.

"Nope. Always wished it was you."

"Wow. Speechless. Didn't think you ever noticed me. TBH."

"Scarlet, we all noticed you. You were just too good for us, is all." And with that, he opened my world to the possibility that I might still be considered attractive to someone. So many years of feeling like I was nothing but average, not worth seeing as anything more than just a mom. I shared that with him.

"Just a mom? That's quite possibly the sexiest thing a woman can be...unless she gets lost in it," he wrote. "Did you get lost?" he quickly asked before I could reply.

"I loved being a mom..." I hesitated to confess the next part, not knowing how he might respond, without wanting to sound forward or conveying a sense of being open to opportunity.

"But my marriage got lost." There was a long pause after that. I wondered if that was too much.

"I get it. We can all get lost sometimes."

"I'm sure it was hard with Darla." I assumed that was the relationship he meant.

"Ha. That marriage was a trainwreck." He ended it with a laughing emoji. I wonder if the Carter I remembered had a sense of humor in high school. He was smart. He was your typical goofy high school boy; that made him funny. I was impressed by how well he could string a series of intelligible words together. He was cute, and he was kind. Back then, more didn't matter to me. But now, I was seeing an intelligent, sensitive man. Was that even something we knew about in high school?

"I don't remember you being funny or sensitive back then...just a cute boy who seemed nice."

"I'm not sure if I should be offended or flattered," he replied.

"Probably a little bit of both."

As the weeks passed before his inevitable move south, we began our emotional affair. There would be no other way to describe it. Our texting evolved from casual conversations and observations about life to multiple daily texts. Our flirting was fun. It was simple and playful but not sexual. It felt nice to do that with a man again. He made me feel good, and I believe I did the same for him.

After a couple of weeks, he texted me asking if he could call me. His text said he was feeling overwhelmed with the move and managing his wife's expectations of how things would be for her and the kids. They were moving for him. He had the opportunity to return to the area and run the San Diego office for a civilian contractor of the Navy. It was ideal. For him. For Nadine, his wife, less than perfect. She grew up in Spokane, which made visits with her family relatively easy from their home in Seattle. She had her friends there. Asking her to leave for his career and the opportunity for a better salary and a bigger house by the ocean, an ocean that was friendly and warm enough to swim in most of the year, took him nearly a year to accomplish. During that time, she had become distant, finding ways to avoid him and focusing solely on their children.

"I need your advice, Scar. I'm second-guessing this moving thing. What if she hates it? What if my boys hate it?"

I was touched that he would ask me my thoughts. "There's always a risk. But how boring would life be if we didn't take risks?" Who was I kidding at that moment, I wondered. I was avoiding risk by staying in my marriage. It was safe. It was familiar. It was empty and lonely, too. But I had become accustomed to those things. The risk for me was in leaving, being alone, and wondering how I would get along on my own again after thirty years of being with someone who made my life easy.

"Very boring," he replied. Three dots followed this. Then they disappeared, then reappeared. He was typing something, erasing it, or at least not hitting send.

"Too many dots. Just ask." I finally said.

There was a long pause with a blank screen that simply said "read" underneath what I had sent him.

"What if we get there, and I realize I am there with the wrong woman?"

"I don't understand." At least, I wasn't sure I wanted to understand because that would have meant he was considering me.

"There's no denying you and I have a connection."

"Yes. Old friends..."

"We weren't really friends then. You said it. But I think I missed out on not being your friend then. It would have been so easy to fall in love with you."

I held my phone in my hand, staring at those words.

"Call me tomorrow. Anytime in the morning after 8 is good."

Carter called at exactly 8:01. I had barely started my second cup of coffee. I could have used an entire pot. I barely slept thinking about what he wrote, hoping this was just an extension of his flirting, that he didn't mean anything by what he said. But there was something in his tone that told me otherwise.

I let the phone ring four times before answering. I suddenly wondered how to answer. "Hello? Hi? Hey? This is Scarlet." *What was wrong with me?* I wondered. It's just a phone call.

"Hey, Carter," I finally said.

I could hear him chuckle lightly before speaking. "Hey, Scarlet. It's been a long, long time." I heard his voice, wondering if I would have recognized it, realizing it was a man on the other end, not some teenage crush. Of course, his voice had changed. And inside, I could feel myself melt a little at how sexy his voice was. It was deeper, controlled, and even a little melodic. It soothed me. And any residual teenage crush apprehension I had of talking to Carter dissipated.

We eased into a conversation that would last nearly an hour. He shared an abbreviated life story: engineering degree, career pilot in the Navy, retired into civilian service in the Navy, and married the second time much later. "I was licking my wounds after Darla. She made me gun shy," he said, laughing.

"Wow," I finally offered after digesting his words. I don't think I gave Carter enough credit for being more than a pretty face all those decades ago. Even as a relatively mature, self-aware teenager, I'm not sure I would have had that ability. He was just a boy I crushed on.

"You've had a pretty remarkable life," I said.

"It's been good."

"How'd you meet your wife? Nadine? Right?" I was curious. I sensed something when it came to their relationship. I knew enough that genuinely happy men don't have casual conversations laced with flirtation.

"By accident." He laughed. "Seriously, she rear-ended me."

"That's funny."

"It was. We exchanged numbers. Shared insurance information led to a first date. A year later, she was pregnant, and I had to be done licking wounds. We got married. That was fifteen years ago."

"And look, it all worked out."

There was silence on the other end of the phone. And I knew.

"I'm trying. We're trying. This move isn't helping. She's resentful. I stayed in that area for her. Longer than I ever thought I could tolerate the northwest. We'd always talked about coming back to So Cal. I belong there. It's where I feel I'm home." I could hear him finally take a breath, like he'd been holding in the reality of his marriage and needed to pour it out.

I didn't know what to say. My mind was racing.

"That was a lot, I know," he said, breaking the silence. "Sorry to dump."

"I wasn't expecting all that," I admitted.

"It's easy with you, Scarlet. So easy. I feel I can tell you anything, and you'd get it."

"That's flattering. Especially coming from you, Carter. God, I crushed hard on you in high school." I paused. "If I weren't a married woman, I'd be crushing on you now, I fear."

Silence.

"You happily married?" he asked.

Silence. Processing how to answer that question.

"Resigned," I offered.

"God, that sounds like you're on death row."

I laughed when I heard those words. I knew Shane took comfort in the routine. He didn't like taking alternate routes; he preferred the road well-traveled. We could have explored many alternative routes together over the years, but my suggestions fell on deaf ears.

"I have no regrets. Shane and I have been together for thirty years. We're routine. We made amazing kids. We just see the future differently. And I'm trying to convince myself that I'm too old to think it can be better than this, that I might deserve more. So, yes, I'm resigned to believing I am lucky to have everything I do, even if I feel incomplete."

Silence.

"That was a lot, I know," I said, half joking. "Sorry to dump."

"I wasn't expecting all that," he laughed as he said my words back to him. "Maybe we both deserve more than we're letting ourselves be open to."

With those words, Carter had opened a part of my heart that had been closed: the part that said you're allowed happiness, to feel warmth, love, and joy, to find meaning in another human, and to have them open to seeing you, all of you, and recognizing you deserve more.

"Maybe," I finally offered.

"Maybe we can find it together, Scar? We could be less lonely together.

"What are you saying?"

"I'm asking you to consider me."

"Are you asking me to have an affair with you?"

"I am. If you're open to it. There's something between us that feels it needs to be explored."

I did not hesitate. I knew I wanted this. Not because it was Carter. But because I had been so empty in my marriage for so long. My ego needed validation that I wasn't some old, haggard woman whose value had long diminished. I likely would have jumped and said yes to the first man who asked me, showed interest in me. I knew that sounded desperate and trivial, like I had no self-esteem. Parts of me did. But the one where someone saw me did not. Knowing another man could be interested in me after years of emptiness required an immediate response: "Yes."

"This will be fun."

"Fun," I repeated, waiting for regret to start filling me. Or guilt for agreeing to be unfaithful to a man who gave me a beautiful life. But I was not feeling any of that. Yet, at least.

"I'll be there in two weeks. Let's find a place to meet. Maybe you can remind me of everything I've missed these many years." The statement is filled with innuendo.

"That's a loaded statement," I toyed back.

"It was supposed to be." My heart skipped a beat.

"I'll see you then."

FIVE

CARTER and I would embark on two weeks of lustful sexting. It was thrilling, naughty, and liberating. I had not felt my body respond physically to the thought of another man since Shane – decades ago. Those feelings long buried.

My marriage had run its course. It had been steady without many hiccups. Shane and I managed our life together like a perfectly laid-out plan. We had yet to consider what a future with just the two of us looked like. We had planned on retirement, in those words. But we didn't discuss what it meant for us as a couple: would we travel more, seek out new hobbies together, or rediscover the parts of our relationship that got lost raising our kids. We never once openly questioned whether we would like each other, the people we had become over the years. So long ago, we stopped seeing each other as husband and wife, as life partners, instead only as a person taking space. If I had broached the subject with him, he would have laughed it off. I might have been accused of overthinking, that things will work themselves out, that we'll find our way. We had managed thus far; we could manage retirement, too.

I let Carter into my marriage. It was cathartic to share with someone the sadness and loneliness I felt. Conversations with my small friend group were shallow like that. Somehow, we all knew that none of us had perfect marriages. Still, those conversations were fleeting references quickly usurped in our day-to-day trials and triumphs. Maybe we were all too recently empty nesting, still trying to grasp what a future sans kids looked like, to open our eyes to the loneliness in our marriages. Or maybe I was the only one to feel these things. I knew that wasn't the case, but second-guessing myself was second nature, especially regarding my marriage.

I did not second-guess Carter.

He offered kind words of support and insight from a man's perspective—a divorced man's perspective. His loneliness was different from mine. If I thought hard about it, I could remember feeling the same way at times when Shane and I were going nonstop raising the twins. That feeling would quickly subside, lost in the realization that my life was on constant autopilot.

After two joyous, emotionally charged weeks, we had finally made plans to meet. He would arrive in town a week before the rest of his family to secure housing and set up his kids in school. He was excited to be moving home, recognizing he could enjoy the time alone, reacquainting himself with his roots before his family arrived. And, he could have me.

Of course, the more considerable burden was on me. I had been living here all these years. I knew people. People knew me. People knew me with Shane. Being discreet would be challenging.

We agreed to meet in Del Mar, a quaint, high-end beach town a few cities away from Oceanside. I chose a smaller, intimate restaurant that would give us privacy and discretion. Lunch at noon, we said. And then an afternoon at one of the small boutique hotels in the area. "Let me pick it," he said. "I want to surprise you." Should I have known then that there was the slightest chance he would renege and get cold feet? If I should have, it was buried deep enough not to surface in those moments.

That morning, I said goodbye to Shane. He never kissed me goodbye anymore, and he never kissed me hello, either. Kisses are long gone. I immediately thought of kissing Carter and what that might be like. I was lost in that thought.

"What about it?" I heard as I suddenly realized Shane was standing in the kitchen doorway.

"Sorry. What?"

"Man, must have been some thought."

"What? Why?"

"I haven't seen you smile like that in a long time."

"I was just thinking about my last conversation with Emily," I lied. "What did you ask?"

"Do you want to get dinner tonight? They just opened the new brewhouse downtown. Thought I should check it out." I felt heat rise in my face.

"I can't. You go, though. You always know someone."

He was irritated. We didn't go out much anymore.

"You always say we don't do enough together. Now I'm asking, and you're saying no," he said, frustrated.

"I made plans today and am unsure when I'll be home." I wavered, "If I'm back in time, I'll text you. But don't count on it."

"That's fine. I'll make it a work function and..." He paused. "Whatever. I'll make it work without you." With that, he turned around and left, the door shutting louder than usual.

I walked to the front window and watched as he drove away. My excitement rose as I realized I was free to get ready for my meeting with Carter. I walked upstairs, showered, straightened my hair, put on a small amount of makeup, and dressed in my favorite summer dress with a simple lace bra and matching panties. The dress was figure-flattering enough without being age-inappropriate.

I knew I did not look like Carter remembered me. I had wrinkles and rogue gray hairs that appeared before my five-week coloring. I was still fit. The swimmer in me never fully retired. I would stay active as a Master's swimmer throughout my adult years. Ocean swims were my favorite. Being in the water made me feel whole, emotionally and physically. I was grateful for how it allowed me to maintain my physique without the hours spent in the water of my youth.

I quickly glanced in the mirror when I was done getting ready. A more extended look would have produced questions and doubt. I grabbed my phone as I was headed out.

"Heading to Del Mar. See you soon." I added a kiss emoji.

He sent a thumbs-up. I waited for more. But it did not come.

I got to the restaurant a few minutes early. I was equally nervous and excited that we were finally making this happen. Lunch and then an afternoon of passion.

The hostess showed me to the table I had reserved. I took the menus from her, pretending to read one of them, but I was too distracted to see the words in front of me. After a few minutes, I anxiously began looking at my watch. Ten minutes passed, then twenty. I checked my phone for messages. There were none.

Carter walked in a half hour late and sat down across from me. He did not make any attempt to hug me. It felt cold. Despite that, my heart skipped finally having him in front of me. I had been anticipating this moment for two weeks. We had both been looking forward to this. But I could tell something wasn't right. His handsome face with steel blue eyes was covered in tiny beads of sweat like he was nervous. He wiped his face and rubbed his hands on his pants. On his left hand, I saw his wedding ring. I had left mine at home.

"Sorry I'm late," he finally offered.

"That's okay. The waitress probably thought I was making you up." I tried to break the ice with a bit of humor.

He fidgeted nervously.

"I'm sorry, Scarlet." I felt the color drain from my face before he could even finish.

"You can't," I said before he could.

"I have too much to lose." He looked sad. Defeated.

"We all have something to lose, don't we?"

"You've raised your family. It's different for you."

"You're right. We're in different places." I had known this all along. I allowed myself to believe he could look past it and take that risk for me.

"You could wait for me?" he had the nerve to say.

"Why would you start this, Carter? Why would you consider me if you couldn't walk away from what you had?"

"I got caught up. I'm sorry."

"No. I think you liked the power trip. I think you liked what you could do to me. I think it made you feel better than me." I desperately tried to contain the mounting disappointment.

"That's not true. Jesus, Scarlett, I wish I could. God knows, I have thought about you so many times over the years. I've wondered what it would be like to touch you." He reached out to touch my hand, but I pulled it away before he could.

I was feeling snarky and had to bite my tongue. I wanted to sarcastically ask him if I should commend him for putting his family first, knowing that the children would grow up and leave home. They don't go, though. They never really do that.

"What if, Carter, the biggest thing you're losing is not knowing if we should be together? And now you never will know."

He didn't say anything. I took a deep breath of composure.

"I get it, though," I continued. "A man loves his wife because she gave him a family, a place to call home. You owe her that."

With that, I got up from the table, and he watched me, unable to speak. He looked sad. I felt a small bit of vindication by my words. He didn't pick me. And I knew why. It wasn't because of me. It was because of the life she gave him. It was because of her.

I felt him grab my arm, and he looked at me. Finally, he spoke: "You're right. I owe her. I owe her whatever respect she can still give me now."

I leaned in and gently kissed him on the cheek. "I'm glad you owe me nothing."

I walked away, not looking back, as I felt him watching me, burning a hole through me, knowing full well that our chance was lost. We would never know if what we had could have sustained us and made us happy for the rest of our lives. But I think we knew the answer: We would have been good together.

I got to my car, sat inside, and stared over the ocean. I wondered how much his wife knew of his discontent.

Did she think him capable of cheating on her, entertaining the idea of being with another woman, when he had her? I wondered if it ever crossed Shane's mind that I might be unfaithful before I was unfaithful. I don't think it did. He believed we were happy like we were. I did my thing. He did his thing. And then we did our thing. It was awkward at first when the kids were gone. While they were still in college, their absences were brief hiccups. It was hard to develop actual routines when we were still putting out fires for them, or at least helping them figure out how to do that independently.

However, once the twins graduated from college, made new homes for themselves, and had friendships that made the need for 911 calls to home less frequent, the space between Shane and me began to grow. The things we had in common became less. The stark reminder that we only ever talked about them hit me hard.

Reconnecting with Carter was refreshing. New. Exciting. It might wane over time, too—I knew that—but the conversation was fluid, easy, and intoxicating.

I laugh at myself in the mirror as I recognize this is the second time I walked away from him. Over three decades later. Sober. Wiser. Broken in little, tiny pieces. He did not choose me. And I knew all the reasons he did not were valid. But twice, he did not choose.

At that moment, I felt myself become small. I began dissecting what about his wife made her better than me. It's stupid, immature, and irrelevant, but I did it anyway because my ego had been tampered with. And, at 55, the ego is fragile and confused and doesn't know what it's supposed to be feeling. I had packed my ego away years ago. I never thought Shane wouldn't be enough. I thought he would be the one that would fill me the rest of my days.

Carter changed that.

My phone pinged. "I'm sorry. I couldn't do it. Not to Nadine. Not to my kids." That message was quickly followed by another. "You looked even more beautiful in person."

I felt a wave of sadness.

"I understand." And I did. At that moment, more than anything, I understood that I was capable of more than I was living with Shane. At that moment, I was choosing my happiness and future on my terms in the wake of my heartbreak with Carter.

I picked up my phone again and texted back. "Please don't contact me anymore."

And then I deleted him from my phone. I knew I could save myself from more pain, recognizing how much *almost* hurt. I wanted to beat myself up for being gullible, allowing myself to believe he could want me, knowing full well the circumstances of his situation. The realization that it did not happen was hard; the greater realization, however, was knowing that I had the power to take my life into my own hands. I had Carter to thank for that.

Ultimately, I gave Carter credit for having the balls to end it in person instead of by text. That would have been the ultimate cop-out. I found myself even more resolute after Carter's cold feet. I didn't want to be the "Bridges of Madison County." I didn't want to be that one weekend that would forever change me. And remind me of all that was beautiful about me. But choose the other side. I was older than Francesca was. I wouldn't hold on to Carter because I knew he couldn't. He could be Francesca. Wondering the rest of his life about me. But I wasn't going to bury my heart for him. That much I knew.

SIX

FORTY HOURS driving. 2,700 miles from west to east. Las Vegas, Albuquerque, Norman, Memphis, and Atlanta before closing out my trek in Charleston. Driving across the United States now marked off my bucket list, questioning why it had been on there to begin with.

I had a list of reasons for picking South Carolina once North Carolina was eliminated. It was beautiful. Temperatures are mild in winter and heat in the summer. I loved the heat. And, above all, it was green. I had my ocean. But I would also have green. And, having spent my life in Southern California, I knew that green was something I had been missing.

My impression of the South was always quaint. But as I drove towards the coast, I learned it was just an illusion. It was vast and expansive. California felt small in comparison. Or was it that it was new, unfamiliar, and with that, an uneasy sense of overwhelming? The southern coast felt vast and imposing. It wasn't just the large homes sprinkled on the shoreline. Or the beautiful bridges that seemed everywhere, connecting one part to the next. It was how open and never-ending it felt. It was relatively flat, giving the impression that it went on forever. But as I made my way along the coast, driving through the various towns, I could see why I thought it was quaint. It felt like a throwback to a lost era. It wasn't Mayberry, but a part of me thought community was essential and maybe even guarded. I felt a sudden surge of panic that I might not fit in here. What if I wasn't welcome? I may not have liked the label, but there was no denying I was a California girl. How would this agnostic woman fit in the South where God Bless and Amen were as ubiquitous as hello and goodbye? I thwarted my gut from knotting up, kept my foot on the gas, and drove until I arrived in Charleston.

I spent two nights there before moving to my new place. I had researched my options in the weeks before I left California and set my sights on Sullivan's Island. Site unseen. The pictures looked nice. Rent affordable. Proximity to beach unbeatable. And the real reason, an emotional one perhaps, I chose it for the simple reason my maiden name was Sullivan. I felt it calling me as hokey as that sounded even to me. Maybe it was a way for me to feel like I was going back in time, getting a fresh start on life.

It might have been different if my parents were still alive, but they had both passed away several years ago. I missed them still, but I am glad they did not have to bear witness to my divorce. They adored Shane. Sometimes, I felt they liked him more than me. I knew that wasn't true. He wasn't a target of my mother's judgments, which were meant to be seen as a form of constructive criticism. Dad would simply reply, "She means well." My brother and I would laugh at this. The older they got, the more life wisdom she wanted to impart, making my father shake his head and silence his voice. But they did adore each other. I could see that. I am glad they did not have to deal with the emotions of my divorce. And that I did not have to deal with added comments on '*marriage is forever*' and '*everyone hits a rough patch.*' Or being accountable to God. I was accountable to me. Mom would have had a hard time with that.

I recognized moving across the country would be challenging. I had fleeting moments of panic as I drove across the country playing Tom Odell's "Another Love" on repeat. There was something so emotional and empowering about that song. It kept me sane. I could sing along at the top of my lungs at a volume louder than my voice, so my often inaccurate vocals went unnoticed by passersby or my invisible passenger.

I knew it wasn't moving to South Carolina that scared me. It wasn't starting over in a new place with no friends. I loved being somewhere new, able to leave my baggage neatly packed away. I had to be honest with myself, though. It was the older part of the story that scared me. The part of my life where I know I don't wow a man with my looks if I ever did that anyway. Or with my hot body. Not that I had one of those, either. I was an ordinary woman. No part of me made me prettier or more attractive than the average woman. I wasn't overweight. And I wasn't overly thin. I wasn't super tall, and I wasn't short, either.

I chose not to color my hair during the pandemic. I decided I could live with the shades of white and grey woven throughout my otherwise dark blonde hair. The wrinkles were there. Botox was once a friend. In this new state of financial affairs, I would ask myself how important that was. To my psyche, it meant a lot. It was a superficial way of hiding what I knew was there for a little longer like I could stop Mother Nature from invading my skin in full force. It wasn't as if crepe skin hadn't slowly started making itself known. Or my little eyes disappearing when I smiled. I was too self-critical, I told myself.

But I knew my story was not about the superficial part of feeling attractive, especially to a man. I wanted my story to be where I got to be unapologetically me, where I could do all the things I had wanted to do for so long without worry or remorse. Shane could no longer look past the woman who cheated on him. His constant questioning in my day-to-day life told me he would never trust me or even forgive me for what I had done, even if he said he could. I knew doubt was always ready to pounce, that there would always be a small part of him that questioned when I went out with friends or visited one of our children. The fact that he suggested a one-night stand would have hurt less told me he understood the magnitude of the emotional void in our marriage. And he knew he wouldn't be able to deliver on that.

I didn't want to erase my life by moving. It had been good. But I didn't want to start over staring over my shoulder, wondering who might be watching, judging, and inserting their opinions on how I should live my life moving forward. Sullivan's Island was a fresh start. I was anonymous. No one knew my history, the bits and pieces that made me who I am today. I felt lucky to start over with a clean slate, a version of me that was authentic, unapologetic, and true to myself. That was liberating, if not admittedly a little frightening.

I drove by my rental property the day before suddenly panicked that it might be a dump, but it was not. The outside was even more adorable than the pictures. An ocean-view cottage had always been my dream, and I was excited to live it for however long I could. I wasn't sure where I would end up, but I liked how this beginning felt.

As I drove around Sullivan's Island, I admired the mix of homes on tree-lined streets. There were gigantic, newer homes and smaller, weathered ones tucked between. Some had beautiful ocean views, while others had trees filled with chirping birds. There were tennis courts, small family-owned restaurants, and even a library. There was an equal opportunity to explore the community while being simultaneously anonymous. I cautioned myself on that note, though. A town this small likely only afforded anonymity for a short time. Or maybe everyone minded their own business. I could only hope.

As I drove the narrow residential streets, I noted the station markers at the various beach entrances. I wondered why some were marked with a half, and they didn't appear sequential. I stopped at the lighthouse only to learn it was no longer open to visitors, its perimeter lined with a fence. It was still romantic, unfamiliar in contrast to my coastal upbringing. I felt my imagination come to life as it played different scenarios of times long past.

I was too excited to sleep the morning I moved into my quaint two-bedroom bungalow on Sullivan's Island. I threw the few belongings I had taken out of the car back in. I was meeting the realtor at eight. And the moving truck was coming between ten and two with as much advance notice as they could give, they promised. I stopped for coffee. I tried to eat but found myself too eager to start this chapter. I was ready to move on to this part of my story.

Janice, a thirty-something Southern belle, met me in front of my new place. She was prompt and overly enthusiastic as she gave me a pseudo-hug. "I am so excited to show you this place. I think you'll love it," she exclaimed like we had known each other forever.

"I can't wait," I said, following her towards the front door.

The door opened to my new home. My new life. It felt symbolic.

I walked in and was instantly mesmerized by the remnants of the morning sun still shining through the windows at the back of the house. Beyond that, I could see the water, calm like a lake, in front of me. I stopped to take it in.

"This view alone would be enough," I said to Janice.

"It is special, but wait until you see the rest of it. The owner updated everything, and you're the first to live here. I think you're really going to love it."

The house was small—two bedrooms, two baths, and a cute kitchenette. I didn't love cooking anyway, and a gourmet kitchen would have made me feel guilty, like I was supposed to want to make food. I was cooking for one these days, which meant not having a plan. I could make leftovers last for three meals. I heated them up and found joy in the ease of it. After years of cooking for my family, it was a relief not always planning meals.

After fifteen minutes, Janice was gone. I was relieved to avoid chit-chat. I watched as she got in her car. She began to back out but quickly hit the brakes. She flung open the door and scurried towards me, waving a flyer.

"Shoot. I forgot to give you this." She handed me the paper and said, "My mom is part of this book club. She's divorced, too. I might have mentioned you to her. Not that I'm assuming you're divorced, but..."

"I am," I offered.

"Oh, good," she fumbled over herself. "I mean. You know what I mean?"

"I do. It's all good. I am happily divorced."

The statement caught her off guard. "Oh. Well, even so, you might like to join them."

It was strange of her to say that. She waved to me as she hurried back to her idling car. I looked at the flier more closely. "Divorced women's book club. A safe space. 5pm at the Sullivan Island Public Library." Some books were listed, followed by the disclaimer that they might choose others "with due notice." I told myself this might be fun. It would be an excellent way to meet some of the locals. At this age, meeting people and making friends was challenging.

Close friendships have eluded me over the years. I stopped trying to figure out why. Shane would say I could be overbearing. I scoffed at that, but deep down, I knew he was probably right. I was a go-getter when I worked and when I was a stay-at-home mom. If you wanted something done, I was your person. I tired of taking the initiative to be friends with other women. Until the kids were older, I didn't feel I was missing anything. But now I yearned for the companionship and conversation of friends.

I looked at the flier again. The next meeting was in a few days, and the next book on the list was "Long Enough to Love You." If that wasn't right up my alley, I thought. At least the divorced women's book club occasionally read books about divorced women. I was relieved that the list did not include Nicholas Sparks. Maybe he wasn't spicy enough for these women. Looking at the few books on the list, I was pleased to see that the only Colleen

Hoover book was "Verity." Emily read her books for fun because "everyone is reading them," she said. "Gotta understand better why she's so influential." She looked at me sheepishly, "Seriously, I'm not getting it. But I keep reading them, so there must be something pulling me back."

"I've read a few. I struggle with second chance romance when you're in your twenties."

"Right? I'm still looking for love number one," she mused.

"Oh, Emily. You had Evan. And Josh. And.."

"Okay, Mom. I get it. I'm not going to settle. And I'm never going back to one of those *boys*," she said, slowly enunciating the word boys.

The list looked safe enough. I could read a book every couple of weeks, and I had already read the first two on the list. I felt armed and ready to walk into a group of women I did not know with the knowledge that I had read the books and could converse about them. At that moment, I made the mental commitment to check out the divorced women's book club. No one knew me here, but it could serve as my new beginning for making friends.

I was all too familiar with the notion that friendships had a new meaning as we got older. The routine of friendships as a function of the kids' activities was no longer relevant. Creating, finding, and making friends was now relegated to my life's situation. I convinced myself it would happen organically as long as I could find the right women to surround myself with. The book club women were divorced like me. It meant they probably had experiences like mine. I would be with my people. I was feeling good about this next step. I would meet women in a setting that gave us all something we had in common.

I PUT the flier aside as a reminder to find my copy of the book and then began unloading my car. I schlepped the few boxes I had into my unfurnished living room. I moved my bags with my clothes into my small bedroom. The queen mattress I had splurged on was being delivered in the early afternoon. I began hanging up my clothes while I waited for the movers to arrive with the rest of my life. The beach cottage was small, yet I wondered if I had enough things to fill the space. It had been a week since I watched the movers drive away with my life, and now I couldn't even fully remember what I had put in there anyway.

The closet faced away from the giant slider that led from the bedroom to the back. I finished hanging the things I could and stowed my bags in the closet to finish later. Parts of me wanted to be in a hurry to unpack; the other parts recognized I shouldn't hurry the newness and opportunity of creating a place uniquely mine. I liked making a home with Shane and the twins. That brought me joy, too, but there were always other opinions to consider. This was me. This was all mine.

I walked to the sliding door and opened it, stepping outside. I took in a deep breath of fresh ocean-laced air. It was warmer and muggier than Southern California. But it was the water that mesmerized me. As it always does. Water calms me. Being near it brings me peace. Water commands my respect. It is power, poetry in motion, beauty in its madness, exquisite in its silence. Water is all-encompassing. Its proximity will always be paramount to the place I call home. It's how I picked South Carolina. I didn't want the retirement communities and "snowbirds" of Florida, and Nicholas Sparks had long made the expectations of North Carolina too great. While I may believe I deserve a happily ever after, I was hoping for happily moving forward. Looking out over the water, I felt a sense of relief throughout my body. This felt right. This felt like the place where I belonged.

THE MOVING truck arrived promptly at ten. They were done unloading and driving off by noon. The mattress came shortly after that. The pieces of my old life fit nicely in the landscape of my Sullivan's Island beach cottage.

By evening, I had moved the essentials into place. I found my stemware and the bottles of my favorite wine I had packed to start this adventure. I opened the Frank Family Pinot Noir. I carefully poured, catching the lone renegade drop of liquid with my index finger as it dripped down the side. I licked my finger, enjoying the sensation on my tongue. I grabbed my glass and walked to the back.

The owner had left a small table and two chairs, which I was grateful for. I sat down and savored the flavors as I sipped my wine. A short walk away, the beach was busy with evening walkers and a few children laughing and giggling in the waves. It made me miss the early years with Henry and Emily and those simplistic summer beach days.

I saw families walking with their dogs. I saw dogs running ahead of panicked owners. I missed Zero. He would have loved it here. I wondered if I should get a dog but quickly talked myself out of needing any unnecessary responsibility as I navigated my new home. I noticed women and men of various ages walking alone. I wondered how many of them were like me, contemplating their life. Were they scared? Excited? Ambivalent? Whatever they were thinking, we were alike in seeking the comfort of the ocean to help us clear our minds.

The beach was my place growing up. I would go to draw or write. If I didn't want to deal with my parents, I'd drive to the coast and let myself disappear. As a teenager and college student, I worked as a beach lifeguard in the summers. It was an excellent job with many cute boys and an opportunity to party. I had fun.

As I got older, though, I didn't head to the water as much. But I knew it was there. For me, there was comfort in that. When I was younger, it gave me peace of mind and allowed me to shut off the world. Maybe it even gave me direction. It serves that purpose today. Literally and figuratively. In California, it tells me west. It tells me I'm not lost. I can find my way -always- if I know where the water ebbs and flows. So, moving east meant changing my compass. There was still water, and it was familiar. I knew it like the back of my hand. It was like looking at the reflection in the mirror where things are flipped. East was my new west. Sunrise, my new sunset. They were both a sight to behold. I needed water like I needed air. That much I knew.

I allowed myself two glasses of wine. I was exhausted. Too tired to go get food. Too tired to make something from the few grocery staples I had. I grabbed the box of Ritz crackers, devouring an entire sleeve. The sun had set, and sleep was finding its way quickly. I put the sheets on my new bed. I showered, enjoying the strong flow of the water against my body. I threw on a T-shirt, brushed my teeth, walked to the cottage to lock the doors, and found myself on my bed. I looked up at the ceiling and then turned towards the water as I heard a wave crash softly. I smiled. "Home," I thought.

SEVEN

I **WOKE** up the following day and made a cup of Nespresso, which I drank black since I did not think to fill my refrigerator with basics. That would be a top priority on today's to-do list. Nonetheless, I savored every sip as I sat on my back deck, taking in the morning sunrise with its brilliant orange hues dancing on the water. I loved that I could open my back door and be within walking distance of the ocean. I was desperate to feel the contrast of the Atlantic to the Pacific, the ocean that had filled my soul and provided solace in moments I needed it.

I reflected on what made the pull to water so strong for me. So many parts of it formed this collective love.

As a child, I remember wishing I was a mermaid so that I could hold my breath longer. I loved looking up as the light shone down, breaking the surface in perfectly dispersed rays strong enough to penetrate with their light. I was mesmerized.

As a swimmer, I appreciated the silence the most. I loved doing a turn, leaving the wall on my back, dolphining as I stared up towards the sky, my bubbles breaking the surface, reminding me the silence was temporary. It was what most struck me when I learned to scuba dive. The silence remained, and the majestic beauty accompanying it while looking up towards the light reflecting its rays through the water was mine to relish for long moments. My mind was closed to outside thoughts. I embraced my inner mermaid in those moments.

I got up from my chair, drinking the last few drops from my cup. I needed the water almost as much as that cup of coffee. I quickly went inside, threw on the first one-piece swimsuit I could find, and headed towards the water. At first, I walked. Then I felt the excitement, and my stride hastened. The anticipation of jumping in the ocean. Not sure how I might land. Feeling the water. Breaking the surface. Falling beneath the depths. The turbulence. The effort to get back up for air. But also the silence. The weightlessness. The strength to surface. To find air again. To breath.

The water was warm, and there was little surf; it was just a gentle surge inviting me in. That differed from California, where the water was always just a little chilly, and some surf was always present. I walked out deep enough to dive under the water, feeling it envelop my body. I swam several yards before turning on my back to look towards shore. And then I closed my eyes and floated.

I loved the weightlessness of water. It allowed me to forget everything else around me. I could get lost in my thoughts, knowing no one would interrupt them. A stream of thoughts, sometimes with answers, often just left me with more questions. But I was ready to tackle them head-on by the time I swam back in.

An airplane flew overhead as I floated. I immediately thought of how often I read the 'life vest under your seat' on an aircraft. I wondered if anyone had ever really thought how absurd that sounds? Really. What good is a life vest if it's under your seat, out of immediate reach to rescue you if you need saving? Shouldn't it just be right there in front, easy to grab? Add the whole thing of having to pull to inflate and blow if it doesn't work. Holy crap. It would be no easy undertaking if you actually had to use one of those vests. Shane accused me of being morbid at times. I chalked it up to having an overactive imagination.

I was startled back to reality as a small wave pushed me, reminding me that water is not always calm or predictable. It can change in an instant. It can be stormy. Currents pull. Rips appear from seemingly nowhere. Even a seasoned swimmer can feel a sense of panic trying to stay afloat.

There were plenty of times figuring out this whole divorce thing I just wanted someone to throw me a rescue buoy to save me from drowning myself. Water was the perfect metaphor for my marriage. When my marriage became devoid of depth, when I needed to understand Shane beyond the surface, when I wanted him to know me like that, when I wanted to dive deeper into his emotions, know all of him, floundering in knee-deep water became a painful reminder that he was not capable of swimming in the deep end.

I liked swimming in the deep end.

I FELT INVIGORATED after my inaugural swim. I showered and put on shorts and a tank top. I knotted my hair in a bun, figuring battling my curls in the humidity was unnecessary when tackling tasks on my to-do list all day.

As it turns out, Sullivan's Island was very small. With a population closing in on 2,000 residents, it meant the conveniences I was used to with a Starbucks on every corner, multiple grocery stores competing for my dollars, and Home Depot and Lowe's quick stops on virtually every route were no longer that simple. But I learned quickly that a short drive over the bridge had all those conveniences. I loved the bridges here. They were everywhere, connecting one small island or inlet to the rest of the state. It was simultaneously isolating but afforded connection.

I searched for the nearest grocery and hardware stores and found several less than ten minutes away. Of all the things I had packed, a toolbox was not one. I did not spend much time in the garage when I was packing my belongings. Tools had always been Shane's thing. He was typical in that regard. He liked fixing things and building them. He bought tools in every size and for every application. He eagerly took on home improvement projects and purchased the requisite tools to complete the job. He was good at it, too.

I was not a helpless woman in the least. I knew how to hang pictures and assemble furniture. I could change a light bulb and hit the circuit breaker if needed. Putting a house together on my own was something I looked forward to. I just needed the tools to do it.

I knew ACE was the place, and that was my first stop. I began filling my cart. A friendly middle-aged man wearing a slightly faded ACE vest approached me and asked if I needed assistance. I gave him my list, and he motioned me to follow him as he efficiently navigated the store and put items in my cart. There was little conversation. He'd casually hold up the item, and I would nod. He would wave them at me if there were color choices, and I would simply point to my preference. He didn't question my decisions. He was on a mission.

When he put the last item in the cart, he looked at me and said, "That looks like everything. Can I recommend something?"

"Sure." Until then, he'd been quiet, reserving opinion if he had one.

"I don't mean to overstep, but this is a lot of starter tools. A toolbox would be a good idea." He caught himself awkwardly looking at me. "I don't mean to imply you don't have one."

"I don't," I offered.

"Well, it's on sale. It's the last one. But I think it would be a perfect starter box."

"It's like my starter and finisher," I said, trying to get him to break a smile. He did not. "So, sure."

He walked around the corner and returned with a shiny red toolbox—the kind my dad used to have. I smiled at the memory. "That is perfect," I said as he held it up and put it in my cart.

"Anything else I can help you with?" he asked.

"No. I think I'm good for now. If I need anything else, I know where to come." He smiled at that and pointed to the cashier up front.

"You have a good day now, ma'am."

I felt the weight of age as he called me ma'am. I would have to get used to that part of living in the South where everyone politely referred to women as ma'am.

I walked to the front of the store. I grabbed a container of cleaning wipes and a bottle of window cleaner as I passed them. Standing in line, I noticed the cashier, a young woman, likely in her mid-twenties, stumbling as she interacted with her customer. She was blushing and could barely make eye contact with him. I couldn't see him, but he was tall, with broad shoulders and blond hair, and random curls were popping out from beneath his worn baseball cap. He wore old Converse sneakers, jeans that did not give any indication whether he had an ass or not, and an old Salty Crew t-shirt. He didn't look like a construction worker. His purchase was packaging tape, boxes, and bubble wrap.

"Bye, Sophie," he said as he walked away. He had a nice profile, but beyond that, I could not tell what would make her blush.

"Bye," she mumbled, her face slowly returning to its original pale color.

"You think he's a serial killer?" I joked.

"No. What?" She was flustered.

"I'm kidding. Just usually what you read serial killers buy at the hardware store."

"Oh, haha. No. That's Ben. He always does that to me. I don't even think he knows he's hot. Which," she rolls her eyes, "Ugh, makes him even sexier. He's always so nice, too."

"Well, that's a good thing. Does he know you're interested?"

"God, no. He's too old for me. He's just super cute to look at. And dream about."

I put my items on the counter and tried to catch a glimpse of him through the window. He was long gone. "Well, if I could offer my two cents." I didn't wait for her to consent, "Life is short. You have to take risks or end up wishing you had taken that chance when you had the opportunity long after it's too late. Live life. That's what I tell my kids; they're about your age."

"You must have been the super cool mom when your kids were growing up," Sophie said.

"I'd like to think so, but my kids might have something to say about that." She laughed.

She finished ringing up my items and packed them in my new handy-dandy toolbox.

The first order of business had been a success. I made a stop at a small coffee shop next to the market. While I liked Starbucks, I loved trying coffee from mom-and-pop or lesser-known coffee shops even more. When I walked in, three other people were inside, and I immediately felt their eyes on me. I smiled as I entered. The barista was a sweet teenage girl who spoke in a heavy southern drawl.

"Welcome. What can I get started for you?"

"A medium nonfat latte would be great." I was a simple coffee drinker. I didn't need flavors or sugars or alternative milk products. Straight-up espresso shots with steamed nonfat milk were a little cup of heaven.

"Sure thing." She looked past me towards the person sitting at a small table in the corner behind me. I turned and smiled as they nodded towards the girl. "So, you here visiting?" she asked, almost as if guided by the person in the corner.

"I don't think so," I said. "I just moved here and plan to stay for a while."

"Oh. That's cool. We get so many visitors around here it's hard to know who lives here sometimes." She finished making my latte and handed it to me. "I hope you like it." I dropped a dollar in the tip jar and took a sip to appease her. "It's perfect," I said as I opened the door to leave, not letting her see I had burned my tongue on the scorching drink.

I put the latte in my car, leaving it to cool while quickly visiting the market. I liked lists. I liked crossing things off lists. A new market always presents a few challenges. Things were in different places than at home, but this was a small neighborhood market, which meant I wouldn't feel totally overwhelmed as I made my way down the aisles.

I found everything I was looking for and added a few things I didn't have on the list. I bought some chicken to cook later and a salad to get my greens. That was my mother's voice, constantly reminding me to make healthy choices. I hated hearing it while raising my kids. I knew how to feed my family nutritious meals. Her words made me smile as I remembered how excellent her cooking was and how important she was while raising my family.

I walked up to the front and stood in line behind several people. The man with the blond curls and baseball cap was once again paying in front of me. It is a small town, I thought to myself. The cashier was an older woman and not the least bit affected by him like Sophie had been. He turned to the man behind him in line as he grabbed his bags and said something I couldn't understand. The man laughed and shook his hand. Before he turned away, though, he looked back toward me, caught my eye, and smiled. I turned to look behind me to see who he was looking at, but no one was there. When I turned back around, he was walking out the door. I didn't know what to make of it, but I understood why Sophie was dumbstruck. He was very handsome, with a million-dollar smile and sparkling blue eyes. He had to be in his thirties. I let myself feel flattered that he smiled at me. At least, I thought he smiled at me. I told myself it felt good to be smiled at by an attractive man. And felt bolstered by the knowledge that at least one incredibly handsome, albeit age-inappropriate, man lived on Sullivan's Island.

I made my way home, enjoying the latte that had cooled to a perfect temperature. I unloaded groceries, took wrappers off my new tools, and organized them. I arranged and rearranged my room. I unpacked all my clothes, filling my dresser and closet. I used the extra bedroom as overflow and storage for the parts I wasn't ready to tackle yet. I had time. I was not in a hurry. I decided the extra room would be my creative space to paint or write. The ideas were beginning to percolate in my brain.

By late afternoon, I was exhausted. But also exuberant about my new life unfolding in front of me. I put the tools in the garage and was reminded I had brought my ebike beach cruiser. A pandemic purchase, I admit to not using it as often as I should have. It was fun – and effortless – riding it. I grabbed it, checking to make sure there was even a charge. I knew I could always pedal if it ran out, but it was not my preferred method of riding.

When I turned the key, the three green lights lit up, indicating a full battery. I had a helmet somewhere, but I hated wearing it anyway. I could hear Shane grumbling at how unsafe riding without one on our busy coastal roads was.

I set out to explore my local neighborhood. The streets were lined with beautiful trees and picket fences, some white, some not. I learned that the station markers were for beach access reference. Station 18 had an interesting white and grey tower. I wanted to ride down the sand and boardwalk path to the water, but I resisted the urge and kept riding.

I smiled when I saw girls on the beach, scantily clad in bikinis with most of their asses uncovered, leaving little to the imagination. *Just like home*, I thought to myself. And just like at home, the boys hardly seemed to notice or think much about it. Emily's assertion that women in the South were prudes was not true, although I didn't see many women on the beach. At least, girls in the South were not. I stopped my bike and shot Emily a quick text: "Same ass-bearing suits here as in California." I sent it with a laughing emoji, knowing she hated my use of them.

Riding here was fun and easy. I enjoyed peddling, saving the electricity in case I had to climb a big hill. But I knew there would not be such a thing. As I drove across South Carolina, I recognized that it felt so enormous because it was flat in contrast to the rolling hills of the California coast. It's a common misconception about California. Because we have beaches, people assume it is flat. It is anything but. While its beauty is undisputed, running or biking on the California coast can be daunting. Biking in South Carolina had proved to be effortless.

When I finally returned home, I had convinced myself that I would not be cooking dinner tonight. I rode by a small hole in the wall a short walk from my cottage. I decided to adventure there for a drink and a bite to eat. I would never meet people or feel like this was my new home if I sat in my cottage waiting for people to call on me. I knew avoiding putting myself in awkward social situations would not be an option if I wanted to get acclimated to my new life in South Carolina.

I rinsed off after my bike excursion. Humidity in the South was real, and I was learning it meant showering more frequently and changing clothes more often. I threw on a loose pair of shorts and a plain white T-shirt. My hair went up in a messy bun. I put my phone and keys in my functional yet cute crossbody Emily gave me for Christmas. That felt like a million years ago, even though it was only the start of summer.

EIGHT

THE HOLE IN THE WALL, Edward's Eatery and Bar, was small and quaint. I walked in and surveyed my options. The sign at the door told me to seat myself. Several people were sitting at the bar. I'd say it was a typical crowd for a place like this. But what did I know of typical? Dive bars were not my scene; at least, they hadn't been for a very long time. There was a woman who looked to be in her sixties. She wheezed like a smoker when she laughed. I could hear her all the way at the front. She was chatting up the drunk bald man sitting next to her. Two seats down, a younger couple were very enamored by each other. She threw her head back every time he said something, and he stroked her leg and leaned in for a kiss every two to three sentences. There were five small booths lined up against a back wall. I made my way to one of those, wanting to avoid the awkwardness of the bar.

I surveyed my booth options, picking the one with the fewest rips in the burgundy vinyl bench. I took a napkin from the dispenser and wiped a few remnant crumbs from the seat. The shiny tabletop veneer was permanently marked with circular glass rings. Salt, or maybe it was sugar based on how sticky it was, ground permanently into the wooden grooves. I expected nothing more from a dive bar.

There was one waitress and one bartender at Edward's. They were very chatty with each other. My money said the bartender was actually Edward, and she was his girlfriend. She walked towards me once she let herself finally catch my eye. She rolled them as I motioned for her to come to my table. I was starving. And parched.

"Welcome. My name's Katie, and I'll be taking care of you tonight. Can I start you off with a drink?"

"Is it possible to get a menu?" She pointed to the stack of menus loosely fitted behind the napkin dispenser.

"Long day. Sorry." She gently rolled her eyes as I grabbed one, then surveyed it quickly. Although I was the only customer requiring attention then, she made me feel I was keeping her from others.

"What kind of beer do you have on tap?"

She looked over her shoulder and read off what she could from behind the bar.

"I'll take a Blue Moon. And..." She began to walk away before I could finish. She stopped and turned back around. "Sorry. Do you know what you want to eat too?"

"I'd just like a burger. Medium. With fries and ranch."

"Cheese?" She was curt.

"Cheddar. Please."

"Got it."

She sauntered away. I wasn't feeling overly confident that I would get my food. No less than five minutes passed, and she returned with a large, ice-cold Blue Moon and a glass of water. I think I forgot to breathe the first several sips. It was thirst quenching. And the slight citrus flavor was incredibly refreshing. I took several more sips before reminding myself I hadn't eaten much today, and going hard fast would likely mean a quick buzz that I didn't necessarily need tonight.

I sat back in the booth, taking in the sights beyond the bar. On the other side of a makeshift partition were three pool tables. Several groups of people were hanging out with their cue sticks, sipping beers while they surveyed the action on the tables. I was horrible at pool but could appreciate the level of skill required to play well.

Just as Katie brought me a huge burger, I caught a glimpse of a man with a backward baseball hat as he walked in with his cue stick case. I took a second look and found myself laughing under my breath. As soon as I made the connection of who it was, I heard a loud "Ben" from the group of players.

"Everyone seems to know him, huh?" I told Katie when she returned with the ranch she had forgotten.

"Ben? It's hard not to know Ben." She watched him with a smile on her face the whole time. I observed as she waved to him, and he raised his cue in recognition. It was amusing how this man was in the same place as me three times today. It is a small town, I thought to myself.

I inhaled my burger as soon as Katie left. I tried to eat slower, reminding myself to chew more, but to no avail. I drank my beer even faster. Katie returned with a second beer before I was halfway finished.

"Thank you. This is amazing."

"Something about Edward's burgers makes you eat 'em without chewing. But one beer is usually never enough," she laughed as she said it. "I'm on autopilot with the second beer when burgers are ordered."

"Perceptive." She came by the table often. At first, I thought she was just warming up to me. But I quickly figured out my table had the best view of Ben. And she was clearly smitten with Ben.

I finished my burger and most of my second beer when I noticed Ben walking towards the bar. I tried not to stare, but there were too many women in my few encounters today who found him irresistible. This was my opportunity to get more than just a glance. He was much younger than me, no doubt. Maybe early to mid-thirties. He was confident in his presentation. I didn't think he appeared arrogant, just self-assured. Arrogance grew in abundance in California, and I knew the look well. His backward hat, a favorite turn-on of Emily's, worked well for him, with his light blond curls randomly falling out the sides. His eyes, though, must have been the reason the women swooned. They were an unusual shade of blue, almost hollow, and sparkled when he smiled. He seemed like a happy man, oddly comfortable in his skin for someone his age. He had a nice build with his clothes on. Mentally, I wasn't undressing him, but I could tell by the fit of his t-shirt on his biceps that he was athletic, his abs slightly visible through the white shirt he wore.

I tried not to be obvious in my assessment. I focused on the check Katie had left for me as he walked by. Yet, he managed to catch my eye as I looked up. He smiled and kept on moving. His smile might have been the other reason the women lusted after him. His teeth were perfectly white and straight. He smiled with such a natural ease that it was clearly infectious. I returned his smile before turning my attention back to the bill. As I pulled out my credit card to pay, Ben walked past me, abruptly stopped, and turned around.

"Are you following me?" he said matter-of-factly. He was looking right at me. I was taken aback. Had he seen me those other times today?

"I think it might just be a coincidence. It's a small town. I'm new."

"So at Ace, then the grocery store, and now here, you mean you didn't even notice me?" His voice hinted at flirtation.

"Hmmm. The hat, maybe?" Oh, that might have unintentionally been a little playful in delivery. "Is it possible we both needed the same things, and it was a coincidence? And I was here first."

He motioned to the empty bench. I nodded. He sat down opposite me and made a two sign to Katie. "I'm okay," I said, pointing to the nearly full glass before me. He changed the two to one as I imagined Katie rolling her eyes in my direction.

"New to town? That explains why I haven't seen you before."

"I'm not sure I'm the woman you'd notice anyway. Everyone seems to know who you are. You have quite a fan club here, Ben. It is Ben, right?"

He nods. "It is."

Katie puts two beers on the table. She looks only at Ben. "Anything else, Ben?"

"Thanks, Katie." He looks at me and then back at Katie. "Have you met..." His glance shifts to me.

"Scarlet," I inserted.

She gave me the same cold look she'd been giving all night. "Not formally," she said.

"Well, now you have." Katie rolled her eyes and went back to the tending tables.

His confidence was intoxicating. A few minutes in the presence of this man made me understand why all the women were swooning. He was poised but not cocky. He was handsome in a rugged way, saying *I could get dirty, but I clean up really well, too.* But there was also enough of him left to the imagination. He was not an open book, but I understood quickly why women would want to read more of him.

He got up from the table. "So I just wanted to be neighborly and welcome you to Sullivan's Island," he paused and then slowly, precisely said my name, "Scarlet." Then he leaned into me. "By the way, you are the kind of woman every man notices." He winked, grabbed his beer, and walked away.

I finished paying for my dinner. Katie managed a meager "Thanks, come back again." I don't think she meant it. It didn't matter. Ben, everyone's dream man, noticed me. And that was an odd compliment as I realized it came from a man at least twenty years younger than me. At this age, I appreciated the gesture if a man was willing to compliment me.

I headed outside, looking forward to a quiet evening on my back deck, listening to the waves gently lapping on the shore. Half of last night's wine awaited me in the fridge at home. This was the first night I wasn't feeling like I hadn't done enough to relax and enjoy a quiet evening in solitude. It was feeling real. I had been going at warp speed up until this point. I could finally slow down enough to appreciate this new life adventure beginning.

I felt on top of the world as I walked towards my cottage, my new home. I was here. I did this. I knew I wasn't perfect. I hurt Shane in the process. I didn't care if people thought I was selfish for picking my happiness. I knew some women and men would judge me for being whiny, wanting more, not giving enough, not trying harder. They didn't know the inner workings of my marriage. They weren't familiar with how time and disinterest had created an impenetrable barrier anymore. I was guilty of judging others at times. There was no reason for them not to judge, form opinions, take pity upon Shane, make me out to be a spoiled brat wanting more, being ungrateful for the life I had with Shane. That was all part of why I came east: escape. New beginnings. I was free to be me. I walked lightly in that revelation.

I could hear someone coming from behind, seemingly in a hurry. I moved over to let them pass, holding my key tightly in case I needed a weapon. Sullivan's Island seemed safe, but I wouldn't take my chances. Then, I heard my name in a voice that had become newly recognizable. I stopped and turned slowly to his voice.

"Scarlet. Hey."

"Ben." I paused in an effort to appear cool. I think. I wasn't sure at that moment anymore. "Hey."

"You walk fast," he said, catching his breath.

"I've been told." It was the truth. Shane hated keeping up with me on walks, saying it defeated the purpose of relaxing while doing it. "Did I forget something?" I asked.

"What?"

"At the restaurant?"

"Oh. No. I just saw you leave, and, well, I thought I could walk you home."

I motioned to my cottage, just a few houses up. "I live close. I'm good. Thanks, though."

"Okay," his voice trailed off slightly as if he had been rejected for the first time like he was disappointed. I felt myself suddenly emboldened. In a what-the-hell moment, I spoke before I could let the inner voice of reason tell me to let it go.

"I do, however, have a bottle of wine at home that I could use some help to finish. You do drink wine, don't you?"

"It's beginning to grow on me," he said with a sheepish grin.

As we walked the few houses to my cottage, we spoke in short, abrupt sentences about the weather, the ocean, Katie. "She's hot for you," I said.

"Katie? No. She's with Eddie."

"I thought so."

"But we dated very briefly a long, long time ago."

"I imagine that happens a lot in small towns."

"What? Dating? Hooking up?"

"All of the above," I offered.

"I suppose. I left for a lot of years. I only recently came back. Just got out of the Navy."

"Ever find yourself in San Diego?"

"Of course. Why?"

"I'm from that area."

"And now you're here. Geez. That's a change."

"I needed change."

"That sounds like a story."

"Nothing special." We were in front of my place. "Here I am."

He followed me up the path. I put my key in to open the door. I could feel him behind me. He put his hands on my hips. He gently moved my hair and began kissing my neck. He whispered into my ear, "I've been noticing you all day. Everywhere I went." He drew a line of kisses as he moved along my neck to my other ear. "I was hoping I'd run into tonight. You are so hot."

At that moment, I turned off the voices that said he seemed too young to be interested in someone as old as me. He did not seem to care; he was genuinely into me.

I paused briefly before pushing the handle to open the door. I turned to him, his body not moving as I turned to face him, feeling his breath on my face. I looked up to him. And then I let Ben kiss me in the shadows of the porch light. His hands lightly rested on my hips as he did.

He kissed me slowly at first, his tongue making its way into my mouth in small waves, teasing me, waking up the memories of what it is like to be kissed like that again. He stopped as if searching for a signal to keep going or stop.

"God, it has been too long since a man kissed me that way," I said, making him smile.

"That's unfortunate," he said. "Your mouth is perfect for kissing." Then he kissed me harder, pushing me gently through the door and into the cottage. He kicked the door shut with the back of his foot as he continued to kiss me. He moved to lift my t-shirt over my head, but I found myself hesitating. He stopped.

"I'm sorry. I'm going too fast," he said.

"Maybe. But I like it. It's just been..." I released myself from his embrace and walked towards the kitchen. I turned on the light, dimming it as I did. "I haven't...I just...ugh..." I stumbled over my words as I tried to articulate I hadn't been with another man in thirty years.

"I have been with one man in the last thirty years." I opened the refrigerator and pulled out the bottle of wine. As I turned to the cupboard to get two wine glasses, I found myself asking under my breath, "God, are you even that old?"

He smirked, and I felt I knew the answer before he could say it.

"I don't want to know, do I?" I asked hoping he was older and just well-preserved. I began to pour the wine as he watched me intently. I handed him his glass.

"I, Scarlet, do not look at a woman as a number. I look at her as sexy, attractive, confident. God, you have an air about you that is intoxicating." We both took a sip of our wine, watching each other as we did. He took my glass from my hand and placed it on the counter next to his. He moved my hair away from my face, his thumb stroking my cheek.

"I am older than thirty, for the record. I might have been in Kindergarten on your wedding day."

"God, that's a relief." He laughed. But I meant it. At least he was a solid decade older than my own children, and the reality that he was only mildly age-inappropriate made my hesitation less.

He leaned in and began toying with my nipples. He enjoyed this. "It's just a number. Does it matter if I can do all these things to you?"

I succumbed. It didn't matter. What mattered was that he saw and liked me and knew how to make my body remember.

"I also don't need wine to want you."

"Does that work on women?" I asked. And he laughed.

"You think I'm a player, don't you?" I laughed in return. He began to kiss the front of my neck.

"Of course I do. Every woman in this town knows you..."

"It's a small town."

"And they all seem to stop and notice whenever you're around."

"I'm not sure that's true. I was gone for a lot of years. Maybe they're just surprised to see me."

"So, you're not a player?" I asked playfully, enjoying the sensation of his lips on me.

"If I see something I like, I let it be known." His lips moved down the v of my t-shirt, his fingers moving intentionally along the edge of the neckline. "I like what I see." I let out a suppressed moan when he said that. I pulled him up to me and kissed him.

"Bedroom?" I asked. He did not reply. He simply lifted my shirt over my head. He turned me around, stroking my shoulders, as he made his way to my bra, seamlessly releasing the clasps. He let it fall to the ground as he cupped my breasts in his hands. His hands made their way to my shorts, pulling gently to remove them. He turned me back around and then pulled them, together with my underwear, down my legs. He kneeled in front of me as I lifted one foot and the other out of my remaining clothing. I stood naked in front of him. He kissed along my bikini line, his fingers gently skimming me, playing with me, and then slowly finding their way inside me. I grabbed the counter to steady myself.

"Oh my," I mustered. And then he spread my legs, and his tongue began to navigate the part of my body that had been devoid of sexual pleasure for so long. I felt my legs weakening, fearful they might collapse on top of him. I pulled him up to me, simultaneously conflicted: I didn't want him to stop, but I wanted to pleasure him as well.

I moved my hands up his chest on the inside of his shirt, stopping to gently kiss and nibble on his nipples. He was clearly enjoying it. His shirt fell to the floor as he allowed me to continue exploring his finely formed body. I ripped the button fly, a sound I have always found arousing and began pulling them off, his excitement on full display. I brushed my hand over his erection, which elicited the slightest groan. He went to pull me up when his pants were off, but I resisted. I returned the oral gesture, tasting him, feeling him inside my mouth, sensing the pleasure I was giving him. When he could wait no more, he pulled me up. "Bedroom, now." He grabbed my hand, and I led the way to my room.

It was inaugural sex. First time in my new bedroom. In my new home. On my new mattress. With my new sheets. With someone other than Shane. After three decades, I felt like I was losing my virginity all over again. Except this time, I better understood what I was doing. He lay on the bed as I made a stop in the bathroom. To pee and for reinforcement.

I was hot for Ben. But the sad reality of my post-menopausal body said I do not get wet like that anymore - no matter how hot he may be or how horny I am. The head and the genitalia did not seem to function together anymore. Would he be offended by that? Find it unappealing?

I handed him the tube of lube, and he did not hesitate. He held it up and removed the cap, adding, "This looks like fun." I gave him a skeptical look.

"Lube is everyone's friend; it does not discriminate," I said as he started to rub some on me very slowly. A finger inside here. Another slide in there. I watched as he put some on himself. He was hard and ready. "This is the fun part," he said as he moved on top of me and then slid inside of me.

His movements were slow and intentional. This felt new, different. Was it that he was younger? Was he more cognizant of a woman's needs? How did he know exactly how to move inside me, tickling the holy grail of orgasm that was often overlooked? Or was it that I was older, knew my own body better, and was free to be uninhibited in bed?

Not that I was with Shane. But we grew into each other, learning along the way what worked. But I wasn't vocal with Shane. Nor was he with me. It was how we had sex. It was a function of our dynamic together. But now, I was open to being anything and everything I wanted in a bedroom. If I wanted to moan and groan or ask for something, that was going to be how sex would work from now on. I had thought about that often in recent months, convincing myself that if I ever had sex again, I was going to be an unincumbered woman.

I was being that. And enjoying it thoroughly. Until this sense of panic hit me. I was suddenly struck by the reality that STDs might apply to me now. Holy shit. You don't really think of it in these moments. I can't get pregnant. Sex until menopause bore the occasional reminder I could possibly get pregnant. But Shane had a vasectomy. Thinking about pregnancy was a long gone thought. I never thought about an STD. I hadn't thought about that since college. But now I'm suddenly hit with sleeping with a younger man whose sexual history I don't want to know. I taught my own children to be responsible. Surely, Ben's parents had done the same. But he wasn't wearing a rubber. I didn't want him to wear one. But still. He wasn't.

"Stop," I blurted out reluctantly. He did. Immediately.

"You okay?"

"Yes. Fine. Wonderful. Seriously, this is amazing."

"But..." He rolled over to lie down next to me. He played with my breasts as he kissed my shoulder.

"Ugh. That's really nice." Awkward pause. "You aren't using a condom."

"Oh. So you're just recognizing that I might be a man whore full of disease, and now I've passed it on it you?" He tried to suppress a laugh as he said it.

"Well, when you say it like that, yes. I might not have said man whore because then what does that make me since it took me all of a few minutes to be lying here naked next to you?"

He sat up, leaning on his arm as he studied me.

"I assure you, Scarlet, despite what you seem to think of me and the women in this town, I do not sleep around anymore." He ran his hand through his hair. "Honestly, I haven't been with anyone in a while. And I was with her for two years before we broke up. So, really, I'm pretty darn clean. And the Navy tested for that shit, so I guarantee you, I'm good. But," He leaned in to kiss my neck, his hand moving inside my leg, rubbing me gently, making my eyes roll, and then he spun me on top of him.

"But," he continued. "Do I need to worry about you?"

I leaned down to kiss him, feeling him move inside me as I did that.

"God, I like this lube," he said.

And for the next hour, Ben and I had sex. We talked. We had more sex. We laughed. And then he said goodbye.

"That was fun." He leaned in to kiss me as he stood outside the door.

"Yes, it was." And I shut the door behind him. I didn't want a false promise it would happen again. I didn't want to become involved with a man twenty years younger than me. I was elated to have hot, passionate sex again after all these years. To know I could still turn on a man. To be seen as desirable. If I never saw Ben again, he gave me enormous confidence in our one encounter.

I went to bed that night content. I didn't allow myself to freak out or panic that if Ben saw me again, he'd be disappointed. Afterall, darkness is the aging woman's friend. But he had seen and noticed me in the light of day. I closed my eyes, thought of Ben's hands moving over me, his lips kissing mine, and fell asleep.

NINE

I AWOKE to the sun brightly streaming through my window. Sunrise over the ocean was relatively easy to get used to. I loved the sunset over the Pacific Ocean, but the sunrise over the Atlantic was equally spectacular. I made a mental note to completely shut my curtains before sleeping. I rolled over toward the light and snuggled the pillow next to me. If I inhaled deep enough, I could smell Ben on the pillow. It was a happy reminder that I didn't imagine it, and I smiled recalling the night before. The way Ben touched me. And looked at me. I was melting all over again.

I sat on the edge of the bed, looking out over the ocean. My new daily routine would include swimming in the morning to start the day. Maybe eventually I'll join a Master's swim program, but until then, a half-hour up and half-hour back swim would be perfect. I liked that I didn't have to hurry to swim. The temperature was constant throughout the day, and the water was always warm. That part would take some getting used to, but I would just remind myself how much I prefer warmth to cold; that morning swims in the Pacific rarely happened because temperatures varied, surfers were territorial, and the familiarity took some of the fun out of the adventure.

After I went for my swim, I took on the task of turning the second bedroom into an art and writing studio. I put up an easel and created a perfect space, looking out towards the water. Inspiration was found in this place. I turned a small table into my desk, complete with my laptop and a printer. I put my files with my ideas on top as a reminder that being creative is how I thrive mentally.

Within the confined space of my little studio, I hung up some of the art I had done over the years as mementos of the joy I got creating. Outside of this room, I would not put myself on display. It felt vain and a little embarrassing. Or, in all likelihood, I lacked confidence in my work. I did not do it for recognition; It was cathartic for me.

The day went quickly, and I felt inspired by my accomplishments. I found myself scribbling words on paper. Poetry. God, I hadn't done that consistently in ages. But the rhythm, the timing, and the joy of telling a story in just a few sentences were satisfying. I finished without re-reading what I had written. I didn't care in that moment. My new life had given me a reason to create again, and I allowed myself to get lost in that moment, in this day.

I also realized I was starving and exhausted. I inhaled a reem of my go-to Ritz crackers, washing them down with the remaining wine from last night. I showered. I had good intentions to read but turned out the lights instead, eager to find comfort in my sheets.

And then I heard a knock at the door. It worried me. I checked my phone to ensure I had not missed an urgent message from Emily or Henry, fearful that maybe the police had terrible news to share. But I had not. I grabbed the heavy-duty flashlight from beside my bed, just in case. I turned on the light as I walked to the front door. I peered out the window, apprehensive about who or what might be there. As I looked out the window, a familiar face waved and gave me an opportunistic grin, saying *I'm back for more.* I smiled and opened the door.

"Ben."

THE NEXT SEVERAL days were a blur. I busied myself with little things around the cottage. I went for swims. And then I waited for the knock on the door that said it was Ben. Ben, who was eager to please me. Ben, who worshipped my body. Ben, who could have any woman he wanted. Ben wanted me. For sex. Because a relationship was not going to happen. Sex buddies, I told myself repeatedly.

But I battled that voice of reason. He was barely older than my own grown children. Ten years, really. That sounded better. A twenty-year age gap was not nearly as incomprehensible as a thirty-year one. I knew I had to be roughly the same age as his mother. That was not lost on me either. *Don't be the cougar* I could hear from inside my head. But he was attractive beyond that. He was intelligent. Introspective. Kind. A good listener. He kissed nice. I loved being kissed by him.

The voice of reason's alter ego challenged society's norms: *Why is it that men can date and marry women decades younger than them, but women cannot? Why is there a social stigma attached to that?* I knew I would never want a long-term relationship with a younger man. It would be fun. I knew that. In my mind, I was capable of age progression. In ten years, I would be gross. I would be really old. And he would be in his prime. I totally got that. But now. Here and now. We were totally, absolutely physically compatible.

While never spoken, it was implied that we both knew our relationship would stay behind closed doors. Public outings and displays of affection were off the table. I did not want the added attention. And I think he liked the covert, sneaking around feeling like he finally had one over the small town of Sullivan's Island.

***

"WHAT'S YOUR STORY?" He asked after we had spent several nights together repeatedly pleasuring each other. He turned to me as I stared at the ceiling. I did not look at him when I answered.

"Newly divorced. Sewing my wild oats." I said.

"You mean repressed oats?" He countered.

I laughed. "Something like that, I suppose."

"I don't imagine either of my parents did that when they divorced."

I was feeling old. But also a little curious. My own children supported me through the divorce. They did not pick sides. They just understood. I turned to him.

"Bitter?" I asked.

"Me?" He gently moved his fingers up my arm, brushing the side of my breast as he did.

"No. Your parents?" I elbowed him slightly, realizing he knew full well what my original question was.

"Mom, yes. Dad, no." He kissed my shoulder.

"He cheated?"

"I don't think so. Never asked. He's too nice. And she's not. I think he just finally grew a pair."

"Hmmm." He began kissing my neck. He stopped as I began to arch my back in pleasure.

He asked, "Why'd you get divorced? He couldn't handle you?"

"Yes. Exactly." He laughed at that. "I'm pretty sure if anyone knew my story, I wouldn't be making friends any time soon."

"Oh. So you cheated? Or wait, you're a serial killer and had to leave town before your crimes were uncovered. No. Better yet."

"Better than serial killer? Really?" I interrupted.

"You were runner-up for mom of the year and took out a hit on the winner," he said, proud of himself.

"Ewww. No. And you don't get to think of me as a mom." I went to get up from the bed, and he pulled me down.

"I definitely don't think of you that way." He rolled on top of me.

"How are you ready to go again?"

"I'm imagining how hot you would be wielding an axe."

This made me giggle. "I wouldn't use an axe. A hammer would be way more satisfying."

"That, Scarlet, is why I find you so hot and irresistible. You are sexy physically, and your mind is off the charts." He looked down at me. "Now stop talking, and let me ravish you."

I motioned to my lips, zipping them shut, watching his eyes light up as he moved slowly inside me. In the back of my mind, I was content that he never followed up with the why of my divorce.

BEN NEVER STAYED THE NIGHT. I liked that. I would never love Ben simply because he was too young. But I loved what he gave me in this transition of life. He made me feel like my body was a shrine to be worshipped. There was no part of me he had not explored except the one I said was off-limits. Even then, he found ways to get dangerously close, making me consider it. Whether he really wanted that or if he just wanted to see how far he could push me, I didn't ask.

It was fun with Ben. We both knew there was no future. Now was when we could fill physical needs that were long overdue for me and heightened for him.

"You could be with any girl, woman you wanted."

"They all want forever. Or a commitment I don't want to give right now."

"Sucks how we can take the fun out of that when we're young, right?" I laughed at my own preconceptions about love and marriage in my twenties.

"You're an old soul, Ben." He was wise beyond his thirty-something years.

"You ever feel weird sleeping with a woman your mother's age?" He laughed at that. His laugh was sexy. Understated.

"I don't have mommy issues. And I don't look at any woman and think of her as a number."

"Okay. That is about the sexiest thing you could say to an older woman." He toyed with my breasts as I said that.

"I like fucking you. You're hotter than any of the other women I've been with." He was not referring to the heat flashes that occasionally made their way into my life.

He thought hard for a moment and rolled on top of me. I could feel him hard against my belly.

"You know what you want. You've figured it all out. I don't worry about pleasing you because you let me know how."

I felt him move inside me and let out an uncontrolled moan. And then he pushed harder and deeper, but slowly, watching me intently as he did.

"I know you like this," he said right before he turned me over, pulled me up to my knees, and entered me from behind. "And I know you really like this." He reached around to stimulate me from the front with one hand while grabbing a breast with the other.

"Yes, I do. Very much." I had never told him that. He read me like a book in bed, remembering the positions and things that had a significantly heightened effect on me. And he knew what was off limits. I'd gone my entire life without anal sex. I did not feel it was something I had missed out on. And I really didn't need to start now. I know he would have liked it. But I had to draw the line somewhere, and I knew that turned him on even more.

I did not let our age difference deter me from relishing the intimate moments with him. Maybe I liked being with him because, in the end, it didn't matter what he thought of me. I wondered if he thought of me as his toy. I know, I most certainly viewed him that way. I enjoyed that.

As the days went on, I also learned to appreciate Ben for the man he was. He was honest with me. He was an old soul in a young body. He had a beautiful mind, a certain innocence not tainted or defined by life's disappointments (yet). So smart. So eager. So willing. A perfect distraction.

BEN DRESSED to head out for the evening. He reached for my copy of "Long Enough to Love You" from my nightstand and looked it over.

"Hmmm. Must be a popular book. My mom is reading this right now," he said.

I grabbed it from him. "You are so lucky we already had sex. The thought of me and your mom reading the same book is kind of cringy." I worked hard to keep the thoughts of me being old enough to be his mom at bay.

"Is it worth the read?"

"I liked it. It's about a middle-aged woman finding her way in the world. And it's for book club."

"Must be why she's reading it."

He got up from the bed. I followed him to the door. He kissed me sweetly.

"Did I tell you I'm heading out of town for a bit? If all goes well, it'll be a new job in a new place. Trial run. So tomorrow night..." He paused and winked at me.

"Got it. I'll be ready." He walked out the door.

And then it occurred to me. I quickly opened the door. "Ben?" He turned around. "I have book club tomorrow evening. Maybe come a little later?"

"Noted." He walked away. I shut the door and suddenly realized that I might be joining a book club that his mom was part of. I was awash in a sudden wave of fear.

TEN

WHILE I'D BEEN PLAYING with my new friend Ben all week, I recognized it was time I made age-appropriate or at least life-appropriate friends here. Ben could not sustain me socially. I knew that. I also knew I could not afford a country club life, so a book club it would be. And why not one centered around women in a similar situation? I'd be able to meet women with similar stories who wouldn't pity or judge my situation.

I had been handed a cheat sheet when the book they would be reading was one I knew well. I entered the library armed with my copy. It resonated with me on many levels, and I felt comfortable conversing about it. It was relevant and spoke to me while I was going through my divorce. It was a perfect book for a divorced women's book club. I was ready to participate and, hopefully, meet a potential new friend or two. God knows, at this age, that was hard to do.

The divorced women's book club took place in the back room of the local public library, eerily named The Edgar Allen Poe Library. It smelled of musky old books sitting unread far too long. A small, dark room that looked more like my elementary school library in the 1970s than the conference-style room found in more modern libraries was set up in an L-shape with hard chairs equidistant apart. The aesthetic was not as warm and welcoming as I had hoped. I knew it didn't matter, but somehow, I convinced myself that a warm room meant a warm welcome.

A group of five women were loosely standing together by a refreshment table that consisted of coffee, water, and a selection of homemade cookies that rivaled any I had ever seen. Two women were positioned to watch the door for the others to enter. I walked in, and half smiled. I did not want to come in like a bull in a China shop. I had that way about me sometimes, especially if I was excited about something. I was more nervous about this, half wanting to turn around, second-guessing my decision to blindly join a group of divorced women discussing a book that likely touched on a few hot buttons. I put on my big girl panties and a brave face and walked in.

I was quickly met by a woman who introduced herself as Audrey. "I'm leading tonight's group discussion. I'm so glad you could join us. Welcome to Sullivan's Island."

The welcome seemed sincere. "Everyone, can I have your attention? I know it's a few minutes until we start, but please, let's get seated. Oh, and I want to introduce you to our newest member," She looked at me blankly.

"Scarlet," I said.

"Scarlet, right." She spoke to me more than the group. She turned to the group, "Scarlet from..." She looked back at me. "Where did you say you were from?"

"I didn't. Hi everyone," I said awkwardly, unaware I was potentially being thrown under a bus. "I just moved here from California." I heard a collective murmur. When I turned to find a seat, the room had filled. I caught a friendly face who motioned for me to sit down.

Audrey pulled out a list of questions and waved them in the air. "Everyone has had a chance to look these over, I'm assuming." She looked at me, realizing I did not have access to the questions. "It's okay," she said assuredly. "If you've read the book, you can participate."

I nodded. "I loved this book. It spoke to me on so many levels." She gave me a look like I said too much. "Sorry," I quickly said, feeling the blood rush into my face like I had been busted for talking in the back of the classroom in high school.

The woman beside me put her hand on my arm and leaned into me, whispering in my ear. "Don't sweat it. Audrey likes order. Throws her off if things aren't according to script."

That made me smile. "I'm Melissa. They call me Missy."

"Scarlet," I said back. "They call me Scar." We both giggled, which, of course, got Audrey's attention.

"Did I miss something, Melissa?"

"Nope. I was just clarifying things."

"Well, alright then. The next question..."

Missy again leaned into me as Audrey's voice droned in the background. "Everyone but Audrey calls me Missy."

I had an instant connection with Missy and was grateful for that moment. Missy looked to be my age, maybe a few years younger. It was sometimes hard to tell. She either colored her hair or was fortunate enough not to gray. It was a pretty auburn shade that highlighted her emerald-green eyes. Her skin was a perfect shade of white, not a tan line on her. She likely spent her entire life avoiding the sun and the repercussions. In contrast, I had spent my whole life chasing it and paying for it now with semiannual trips to the dermatologist.

Audrey looked directly at Missy and me as she posed the next question. She was reading from her copy of the discussion guide, which was neatly displayed in a plastic sheet protector.

"Let's let our newest member start this one off." She looked at me. "Is that alright, Scarlet?"

I felt all eyes on me. I shifted in my seat. "Of course." I wasn't going to say no.

"The question asks: *Do you think men and women define infidelity differently?*" She looked up from the sheet when she finished reading. I could do this. I dug in. I knew my answer.

"I think that's a tough one. Not knowing any of you, but making an assumption: I don't know that even in this room, we could totally agree on what that means. I mean, does having an emotional connection with someone mean you're cheating? Or does it have to be physical?

You could be totally emotionally connected with someone and never touch them. And two people could have sex and never be connected." I saw a couple of women take pause at my response. Others were shaking their heads yes; some shaking their heads no.

"Right. So what's worse? I'm guessing most people choose to define it based on the version that makes what they did seem like the lesser offense."

The room was quiet for a moment. Missy broke the silence.

"I think that makes total sense."

"Of course, you would," someone blurted out from the front of the room without looking at Missy.

"What's that supposed to mean, Margo?"

"Nothing. It's just your husband wasn't the cheater, was he?"

Missy sat up in her seat. I knew there was something that I liked about her.

"Oh, Margo, I don't think a book club is the right place to discuss this. The question wasn't about my marriage. Or what woman may have slid in to fill my spot when my marriage ended." Oh, that was a burn, I thought. She continued without missing a beat, "Physical, emotional. It's kind of all the same in the end, isn't it? For men and women." She gives Margo an evil side eye, causing Margo to look away in disdain.

Audrey attempted to resume order in the room. She looked around and stopped at one of the women, who seemed a safe, noncontroversial member.

"Abby, how about you start off the next question?" She looked up from her book. She was an ordinary-looking woman with one of those mouths that looked like it was always turned down, probably not on purpose, but a sad facial feature she wore. She had a nice smile when she turned that frown upside down. She looked older, her hair streaked with grey, cut shoulder length, and very appropriate for a southern woman of stature. I couldn't tell if she was smug or just soft-spoken. She had an air of contradiction about her.

Audrey read the question from her list, "*Before Tripp happened, Jenn was struggling. She wanted a reason to leave, not just a feeling in her gut. Do you think there has to be a catastrophic moment for a marriage to end? Or can marriages just run their course? Do people change so much that they can't come back? And can one or the other change enough to save the marriage? Ultimately, did you feel Jenn was fair to the process?*"

Abby reflected for a moment before responding. She looked at her copy of the questions as she prepared her answer. "I think there has to be a reason for a marriage to end. They don't just run their course unless one of you quits trying. No one changes that much, and if they leave, it's because they quit and didn't think you were worth fighting for. Jenn should have been kinder to Mark. He didn't seem all that bad." Her response was monotone and sterile.

"Not much emotion in that response," Missy whispered in my ear.

"That felt very high school," I whispered back.

I thought I said it quietly, but Abby heard me. "I'm sorry. Was that answer not good enough for you?"

"I don't think there's a right or wrong answer. It's just an emotional topic, so I guess I expected more depth." Why I said that I don't know. I was trying to make friends, not enemies.

"Well, clearly, you know me well enough to judge my response." Smug. She was definitely smug, I thought.

"I just thought Jenn had conviction. She knew she'd be miserable with Mark. She had an affair, and he didn't even care."

"That wasn't the question."

"No, but the point of the question is to have a discussion, right?" I looked around the room as the women stared at me for taking on Abby, who clearly wielded more power than my initial assessment of her. "My opinion: they were never going to be able to come back because a marriage can be so broken that you can't simply put a patch on all that was wrong and hope it holds. Not everyone has to be a victim. I wasn't."

"Amen to that, sister." I heard Missy say loudly, and a couple of others nodded their heads in agreement. Abby was fuming, and Audrey was unsure how to proceed.

"Well, aren't you special?" Abby finally said. "We should all be so lucky. But not all of us were."

Audrey spoke before I could respond, not that I knew an appropriate one at this point. "Wow, ladies, look at the time. That went quickly. One more question, then I'll lock up, and we'll all meet at Poe's Pub for our usual happy hour."

After that exchange, I wondered what I had gotten myself into. I was looking for a like-minded group of women who had been through what I had: divorce. I had not considered I would be an outcast in my own "community" simply because I didn't fit the narrative of a divorced woman scorned. Instead, I found myself in a community of morally rigid women who were quick to pass judgment, knew better than anyone else what was right and wrong, and were closed-minded to understand that not everything goes according to plan and that not all of us are victims.

Morally rigid. I wondered if I made that word up. It sounded appropriate. They were the women who judged without flexibility, could not empathize with others, and judged simply based on the crime committed without a deeper understanding of those actions. I am not sure it's actually a term. But I liked it. It helped me better deal with those around me who could not see other's situations beyond bible scripture. I do not wear my religion on my sleeve. Even once upon a time, when I would have said I was a Christian, I did not. But time, life, circumstances, youth sports. They all hardened me.

The morally rigid were allowed to ask for forgiveness of unethical crimes simply by prayer. I came to understand – and believe- that whoever is judging me and my life's performance will judge me for my actions rather than my prayer and asking for forgiveness every time I did something unsavory. It is how I came to be an agnostic. With too many beautiful things in this world, like kids, that are hard to explain, I always believed a higher power of some sort had to be responsible. But with so much ugly in the world, I constantly found myself conflicted.

I don't like labels—I never have—but I cannot pretend when I sit among my women book clubbers that I am a good, praying Christian woman. I am a good, agnostic woman. I wear that alongside the scarlet D for Divorcee, which I have emblazoned on my chest. I doubt they would expect anything less.

I stood up from my chair, grabbed my bag, and turned to leave. I felt myself needing air. Missy came up behind me.

"Hey, you should join us at Poe's."

"I'm pretty sure I've made a pretty strong impression already."

"Nah. That's just how Abby is. The rest of us are pretty subdued."

"What's her problem?" I asked.

"She's still bitter about her divorce. "

"Recent?"

"God, no. Many years now. She just can't handle that he's happy without her, and she's miserable not making him miserable." I laughed at that.

We continued to walk out of the library. She tried one more time to get me to join them.

"Really, we don't bite."

"I appreciate it. Next time. But let's grab a coffee sometime."

"I'd love that." She grabbed my phone and typed in her number.

"You really should have the lock feature on," she said as she handed it back to me. There are tons of creepy people around here." She gave me a quick hug before turning to walk away, adding, "I was never a victim, either." I knew I liked her.

The book club had been a mix of so many things. Most of them were unexpected. I left the book club that night with a pit in my stomach. The divorced women's book club was full of women who were not just seemingly morally rigid but also scorned. I was the opposite: Not the woman scorned, but the woman that scorned. I felt like I had a big, fat A embroidered across my sweater. Not a D. It should be a D, right? I mean, I joined the book club for divorced women, thinking we'd all have something in common beyond the books we were reading. They would be my women. My future friends, I thought. They wouldn't judge me because we were all in the same position. But then it dawned on me. Maybe we weren't? What if they were the women scorned...by someone like me? Their husbands' infidelity is the root of their unhappiness. I told myself that was silly. They would not have the dossier of my life before them. I came here with the same scarlet letter they did. A big, fat D.

I GOT HOME from book club and jumped in the shower. I hoped to wash away all I had experienced at my first book club. My mind was spinning. That was not how I was supposed to leave an impression the first time I met a group of my peers. I contemplated whether I ever wanted to return again but knew making a decision now would be impulsive and irresponsible. Besides, I had met Missy, and I liked her. I couldn't remember the next book, but I hoped it would be a silly second-chance romance with twenty-something-year-olds. At least that way, we could all laugh at how unrealistic a second-chance romance was when you hardly knew what love was at that age.

I was more excited than usual for Ben to come over. Maybe it was that I needed a distraction from my own thoughts. I wore a sexy baby doll dress without a bra and no underwear. They'd be coming off anyway. When he finally knocked, he barely said hello when I opened the door as he stared at me in my dress. His eyes were on fire as he looked me up and down, my naked body silhouetted through the dress. I don't think the expression of being hot for someone has ever been better conveyed. He kissed me hard and moved towards the couch, lying me down. He lifted my dress, excited by the lack of underwear, and fingered me until I was wet. The thought that I ever believed being post-menopausal meant not getting wet naturally anymore was not lost on me. I was ecstatic that my body could still get aroused like this. He kissed my breasts while fingering me to an orgasm I wasn't expecting to happen so quickly.

He got up and removed his clothes while I watched. He sat down and motioned for me to climb on top of him. I liked how it felt to move up and down, setting the tempo, and watching his reaction when I let him go deeper. It was fun for both of us until he couldn't hold back anymore and released his pleasure inside of me. I liked watching him in that moment. Ben was confident in his own skin and made me feel confident in mine. It was easy to be with a man you knew wouldn't be forever; he would only be a moment, a footnote in this chapter of my life.

Ben was eager tonight. Maybe he was, knowing it was our last night for a while. I wanted to savor it since I was not sure it would happen again when he returned. He might have an epiphany when he's gone that he had made a terrible mistake hooking up with me, or he might decide it was fun, but now it's done. I'd be disappointed, but I'd have these beautiful memories.

We sat on the couch naked. I was never comfortable doing that, but I liked looking at him as he sat across from me, equally nude, his body perfectly defined and young. Oh, so young. I wanted to cover my belly with its little baby ledge and wipe the sweat from under my sagging boobs, but I knew it didn't bother him. He stared at me like I was perfect the way I was.

"Wine?" I asked.

"You have prosecco or something bubbly? I have an idea for later." He winked at me. I got up from the couch and walked to the kitchen, feeling his gaze on my ass as I walked away.

"Does that idea involve your tongue on my body?" I teased.

"Am I that transparent?" he asked. I pulled a chilled bottle of prosecco from the fridge and popped the cork. I poured two glasses. I walked back to the couch and handed him a glass.

"These are for now. The bottle is for later." I put my finger in my glass and painted a small line just above my nipple. I leaned in for him to kiss my breast.

He tongued my nipple, sucking hard at the prosecco. "I knew that was a good idea."

I sat down, legs slightly open, and faced him. I was being naughty tonight. This was so out of my comfort zone, but strangely, I felt like it was the most natural thing in the world to do with Ben.

"I need to regroup. And you're being so fucking hot. Damn, Scarlet, I am going to miss you."

I took a drink of prosecco, licking my lips. I felt silly, like a grade-B porn star. But also relished that I had this much sway on a man twenty years my junior.

He cleared his throat. "So, changing gears. Just for a moment. How was your book club tonight?"

"Oooph. It was rough. I did not make a great first impression. I need to learn to step back and just observe sometimes. Keep my mouth shut."

"I like your mouth open."

"Haha. You know what I mean. There are some tough women in that group."

"You aren't kidding. Most of them do social things with my mom on the regular."

"Yeah, well, I'm sure your mom isn't as bad as they were."

"You've met my mother. You know she's totally insane."

"How have I met your mother?"

"Really?" he asked. I was stumped. I had not crossed the paths of many women in this town. Except.

"Holy shit."

"Yup." My divorced women's book club.

"Who, though?" Ben didn't bother answering me then. He could tell I was thinking.

My mind was racing. Picturing each woman in the group. Who was the most bitter? Who bitched, complained, and hated life the most? Light bulb moment.

"Abby!" I looked at him as a smirk grew across his perfect lips. "Abby? Really?" Then those perfect lips began kissing my neck, making their way towards my breasts. He was ready for me.

"Holy shit," I said again under my breath. My head was spinning so fast I thought I would puke. He ignored my reaction, somehow finding it amusing, and an invitation to seduce me again.

He laid me down on the couch and carefully began pouring his glass of prosecco down my stomach, sipping as he went, making sure none was getting on the couch. He painted rings of prosecco around my nipples and then drank them in, finishing with a nibble on each side. "I like to be balanced," he said. I just moaned.

The spinning turned to desire as he moved the prosecco trail down my stomach. That equally beautiful tongue of his found its way inside my legs where he had cum moments before. Somehow, I think he liked knowing it was his wetness there, almost like he had marked his territory. He looked up at me, smiled, and then stayed long enough to make me quake again. And all I could think was, "Fucking Abby. She may be a bitch who would hate me if she ever found out. But fucking Abby, her son had a gift."

During our last night together, I realized several things about Ben. He liked sharing his tastes with me. Liked kissing me after going down on me. Liked kissing me after he'd cum in my mouth. He was a plethora of tastes, a perfect cocktail of his fluids and mine. He was an excellent, selfless lover. He was a genuinely kind person. He was Abby's son, which still made me queasy. And, finally, I recognized that I had been selfish: I had no idea what Ben did for a living since leaving the Navy. It made me feel horrible that I hadn't even asked him that simple question, too consumed by lust to even know that.

ELEVEN

I **WAS** sad to wake up the following day knowing Ben was leaving. I had plenty of things to do, I told myself. And it wasn't like I spent my days with him. It was just a few hours in the evening. But still, a part of me felt a little melancholy, knowing I would not see him for a while. If ever again, I cautioned myself. He made me feel welcome here. And after the book club debacle, I was all the more thankful for him.

I woke up to a text from Emily. "Hi Mom. I miss you. I have a few days at the end of the month. Can I come visit?"

I was so excited. I missed seeing her. "YESSSS!!!!" I knew it was too eager, but I loved that she reached out to me to visit instead of me reminding her of the open invitation I had extended to her. My second text was more composed: "Stay as long as you like. Just let me know when."

I got up, made coffee, and headed for my morning swim. I liked the simplicity of my routines on Sullivan's Island. I didn't have to be anywhere, answer to anyone, or, as was the case in Oceanside, fear the proverbial eggshells that Shane and I often found ourselves walking on.

During my morning swim, I made a mental list of things I wanted to do with Emily when she came. I knew she'd be happy just going to the beach, going for runs, and riding bikes. She might humor me with a run. The soccer player in her had an effortless ability to run miles at a fast clip for much longer than I could do anymore. I told myself I needed to look up a bike rental place nearby.

I did an hour swim and didn't think about Ben at all. That was healthy, I thought. It was also a function of Emily sending me a perfectly timed, distracting text. By the time I got back to shore, I had my day mentally laid out.

As I bent down to grab my towel, I was blindsided by a tongue and the wet kisses of a wild-looking, albeit amiable dog. "Hey, big guy. Where'd you come from?" I looked around. In the distance, I made out the figure of a man hustling over. He was slightly winded when he reached the dog.

"Otis, come here." The dog looked at his owner and then turned his attention back to me. The man pulled Otis from my leg. "Otis, sit." He reluctantly did as he was told.

"Otis has a hard time listening. He's got this wild child thing going on."

"I had a dog like that once," I told him.

"Oh yeah. What happened to him? Accidentally leave him on a trail?" I would never have left Zero anywhere. Despite his wild ways, I adored that dog. I missed him all the time.

"Lost him in the divorce, actually."

"Oooph, I'm sorry."

"Me, too. I really liked his wacky ways."

He put out his hand, but Otis jumped between us before we could shake. It made me laugh.

"Otis likes you."

"I have a way with dogs." I smiled.

"I'm Beau."

"Scarlet. Scar for short." I studied him as I said my name. He was an attractive man. Beau was just a little taller than I was. And, odds were, he probably didn't weigh much more either. I was still a version of my old swimmer self: bigger shoulders, thicker build. I was fit, but I was not thin. Beau was fit with a narrow build but had strong shoulders that resembled a man of the ocean. Maybe he had been an athlete once or still was. He had salt and pepper hair that was still full and youthful. I couldn't tell if his disheveled hair was a function of being due for a haircut or the chase he had just been on to catch Otis. Or maybe he liked the grown-out pandemic look even though those days were thankfully behind us. He had a nice tan and a clean-shaven face. His blue eyes lit up when he spoke. An animated man, I thought. For a moment, I caught myself thinking he was an attractive man.

"I've never seen you around here before. You recently moved here?" he asked.

"A couple of weeks ago. I'm renting one of the cottages right up there. Just making sure I like it here before I commit to anything." I pointed in the general direction of where I lived.

He asked where I moved from, shocked to learn I was from California. I could tell he had to refrain from making some sort of joke about it. I appreciated it.

"I hope you're finding South Carolina to your satisfaction."

I did. The people were friendly. I met a man on my first night in town who was satisfying me sexually in every way imaginable. He was not the future. But I liked the sex. I liked how alive he made my body feel, recognizing that my age didn't matter when it came to satisfying each other. We would never be more than fuckbuddies. So crass that way, I know. But Ben was just that. We could laugh and talk about the world, but neither of us would ever be anything more than a passing fancy.

"The people are so nice," I told him. "But that's why I chose it here. Pretentious California was my least favorite part."

He laughed at that. And I caught his eye looking at me just a little longer.

"You thought I was one of those pretentious, shallow Cali girls, didn't you?"

And he laughed again. I liked that I could make him laugh, that he was easily amused, and that his laugh was infectious. And it made me laugh.

"No. I'm glad you think we're nice."

Otis darted down the beach when he saw several birds land on the sand fifty feet down the beach. Beau rolled his eyes as he went to chase after him. He stopped, turned around, and said: "I'd love to get a drink. Without Otis. Maybe. Some time." I didn't respond. He could tell I was confused.

"With you. If you'd like."

"Yes. I'd like that." I would very much like that, I thought.

"Then follow me to Otis so I can get your number." He bounded down the beach in hot pursuit of Otis, who was manically barking as the birds flew around his head, taunting him as he tried to grab them.

I didn't run behind him. I didn't want to appear too eager. Other than Ben and outside of my ACE hardware trip, he was the first man I'd met here. And he genuinely piqued my interest. There was something familiar about him, too. But I knew that wouldn't be possible. His accent told me he was a southern man, likely born and bred. Before I moved here, I had not known any authentic Southerners. I found myself lamenting that at times. I really did like their Southern hospitality.

I walked up beside him as he was putting the leash on Otis. He handed me his phone.

"Type in your number."

"I can just get yours and put it in my phone." He looked at me skeptical.

"But then there's no guarantee you'll reach out to me. And I'd be disappointed. I get your number then I know I've at least got a chance of getting that drink with you."

"That's fair." At that moment, I thought this man was charming, forward, and interested in me. And age-appropriate.

He looked at me, towel in my hand, standing there in a bathing suit, looking like a wet dog. "You swim? Or just play in the water?"

"Both. But I like to start my day with a swim."

"I like to end mine with one. Let's go for a swim before we get a drink."

"Hmmm. I don't usually swim with other people." I didn't want to make him feel bad if he couldn't keep up. I never considered he'd be a great swimmer. He didn't look the part. I reminded myself that in all my years of swimming, the older we got, the less we looked like the swimmers we once were.

"I swim at this really cool spot. Meet me in the morning. Station 16. 8 o'clock work?"

This was going fast. I gave the guy my phone number, and now I'm committing to a swim.

"Okay," I said unsure.

"Okay! It'll be great. And if you still like me after that, we can get drinks. Later in the day, of course." Otis yanked hard, and off they went. I stood there, far from where I left the water. I turned and began the walk back up the beach to my place. I shook my head at what just happened, trying to tell myself it was real.

When I got home, I tried remembering everything I told myself I wouldn't forget before meeting Otis and Beau. I'd been awake for only two hours and already had a full day's worth of excitement.

I PARKED my car on the street near Station 16. I woke to a reminder text Beau sent.

"See you at 8. Station 16. (Also, please confirm this is Scarlet so I don't feel like an idiot if you don't show up and some crazy person does.)"

I sent him a laughing face with the added words, "What if I'm that crazy person?"

Multiple laughing faces. "Otis would have warned me." He was quick. I liked and appreciated that.

The trail to the beach was a beautiful walk through lush green trees. I liked all the wooden trails the beaches here had. I imagine it kept people from running all over and ruining the vegetation and animals native to the area. The trial opened to a scenic beach that felt isolated from the rest of the region.

When I reached the trail's end, I saw Beau waiting by the water's edge. He waved to me when he saw me. He was wearing swim trunks and a T-shirt. I could see a pair of goggles in his hand. At least he was prepared.

"Good morning," he said in a cheerful tone.

"Good morning. This is a beautiful spot."

"Little more isolated than some of our other beaches. I like the solitude."

"Swimming is my solitude," I said. It was true. Even swimming with another person, it was impossible to have a conversation. It was another one of the many things I loved about it. You didn't have to talk to anyone because you couldn't talk to anyone.

He took his shirt off. Beau, without his shirt on, was not Ben. Terrible, I should compare. I guessed Beau to be in his sixties. I did not expect him to look like a man in his thirties. I know I didn't. But Beau was confident with his shirt off. He didn't try to hide anything. He smiled at me as I lingered too long on his body. I hoped he didn't think I was assessing him, even if I was. I hadn't taken off my sweatshirt or my shorts yet. Did he expect a thirty-year-old's body? And, hello, you idiot, he met you on the beach in a wet bathing suit. He already knew the answer to what waited under the clothes. And why did I care? I wasn't dating him. I wasn't sleeping with him. I was simply going for a swim with him. Fuck those insecurities that have laid latent for all those years I was married and cared less.

"Come on. Let's go," he said eagerly. I took off my clothes, grabbed my cap and goggles, and headed down to the water. I watched as he entered the water and quickly began dolphining out past the breakers. I wondered if I'd been duped. Most people don't have the first clue how to dolphin out in the water.

We swam hard for an hour. I had not pushed myself like that in a very long time. At the halfway mark, he stopped, and we trod water for a moment. "What do you think?"

"I think you never told me you were a swimmer."

"I didn't? Hmmm." He did not wait for a reply and began swimming back in the other direction.

We finished the swim. I was impressed.

"So, were you holding back to be nice?" I asked.

"Hah. Hardly. I was working hard to impress you."

"Consider me impressed."

"Cool."

"Seriously, do you have a swim background? Or are you just naturally aquatically inclined?"

"Both, probably. I was a swimmer once."

"Like high school?" When someone said they were a high school swimmer, I had to take it with a grain of salt. Anyone could swim in high school. That would not have impressed me or even accounted for how he could swim as well as he did.

"Something like that. I swam through high school. I made Olympic trials in college during my senior year. That was cool. But I was far from what all those other guys could do. I'm not exactly built like a powerful sprinter. And that's what I did. So this long swim stuff is always a challenge to me."

"I'm impressed." I felt the fool for thinking he wouldn't keep up. It wasn't like I was this great former swimmer.

"I'm glad you were impressed. I had to work that." That made me giggle, knowing I wasn't the only one swimming out of my usual comfort zone. "You clearly have a swim background."

"Swam in college, too. No trials. Definitely not a sprinter. I love being in the water. That was the one requirement for moving when I packed up to leave."

"Many people buy the hype that North Carolina is the better choice."

"Yeah, well, Nicholas Sparks kind of ruined that for me." He looked at me funny. "Long story."

"Perfect. You can tell me all about it at dinner." He was charming and quick, not missing a beat.

"Thought we were doing drinks."

"We can start with that. You made me work up an appetite." I laughed.

We walked up the beach, making small talk. He shared some fun facts about Sullivan's Island. He had a pleasant voice that was easy to listen to. He made me laugh and smile. It felt wonderful to be in the company of a man who seemed confident in his skin, which is what I was trying to do, too. That, I had reminded myself, was the beauty of being older. I didn't want to have to pretend to be anything other than who I was. Beau clearly seemed to embody that, too.

WE MET in front of Sullivan Island's newest tap house. I didn't want him to pick me up. I lived close, and if it turned out he was a weirdo, he would at least not know exactly where I lived. I wore a simple summer dress with my hair pulled back in a high ponytail. I was not going to battle the humidity that never dissipated. My hair was going to be wild, even straight, I told myself as I got ready.

Beau approached me. And he kissed me as I went to hug him. Not just a peck but a long, intentional kiss.

"Too much too soon?" he asked. I couldn't hold back the smile.

"Just unexpected. It's been a lifetime since I've been kissed like that." I caught the untruth in that, as I said it. Ben kissed me. But this was different.

"I thought about that. I remember how strange it was to kiss someone other than my wife the first time."

"So you've done this a lot."

He laughed. "A few times. I've been divorced a bit longer than you have. And I was never going to be one to sit at home and feel sorry for myself."

"Me either. Just wasn't sure," I began to trail off. "I wasn't sure if another man could find me attractive in that way again. I mean, God, it's been decades of the same man. The kisses became less. Everything became less."

"Until it became nothing at all," he added.

"Exactly." My marriage had become a fleeting peck on the lips. The kisses were so quick sometimes, and I'm not sure our lips touched. Beau kissed me, and I could feel the residual moisture on my lips.

"That's why I decided I would just kiss you."

"Because you felt sorry for my drought-ridden lips?"

He laughed. "Because I haven't stopped thinking about you, and I didn't want to miss that opportunity if it's the only one I've got."

"Hmmm," I said, toying with him. "So your confidence level is low?" He smiled at me with his eyes as we walked towards the front door of the tap house. Before he pulled the door open, he paused, looked me in the eyes, and said, "Because you are simply one of the most beautiful women I have ever met."

He made me smile. And blush a little. "Is that a southern thing?"

"What?"

"Telling women they're beautiful."

"Maybe for some." He opened the door, and as I walked past him, he said, "But I only tell the ones who truly are."

Dinner was easy conversation and laughter. I learned that Beau had been a fire chief in Charleston. He and his wife divorced when he retired. He could have been bitter about her getting a large chunk of his monthly pension, but he was not. "She raised our kids. She stayed by my side. Then, she became a thorn in my side. It's hard not to cross paths on occasion. We still have some of the same friends. At least, the ones that didn't pick sides. I grew up here. I'm not sure why she wanted to stay." He laughed as he thought about it. "I think the whole thorn in my side is probably right. It does make it easier when our kids come to visit."

"How many kids do you have?"

"A son and a daughter. God, I think they're in their mid-thirties. I try not to remember how old they are for my own sake."

"How old are you?" I asked.

"Direct. I like it. Sixty-five." He looked at me. "Too old?"

"For what?" I asked playfully. "I'm almost that old." He raised his eyebrows. "Okay, in ten years. It's a number. Do you feel like you're old? If your swimming is any indication, I'd say not."

"I feel lucky to be in the shape I'm in. My parents lived to be pretty old, so I think I've got a while genetically." He motioned to the waitress to bring us two more glasses of wine.

"So, the Nicholas Sparks thing. What's that all about?"

"Good memory."

"I pay attention. It's really not hard to with you."

"I'm a sucker for sappy romance stories and happily ever after. All his books seem to be set in North Carolina. I didn't want to move there and be disappointed that sappy and happily didn't really happen in North Carolina."

"You don't think they can happen in South Carolina?"

"I hope they can. But I didn't come here with an expectation it should."

His eyes were always on me. I liked how they looked at me. They were mesmerizing. I would find myself just staring back at them. They were so blue, almost hollow. They made me want to dive in, leaving rippled rings in my wake.

Midway through dinner, I felt a sense of panic come over me. I knew those eyes. I knew them well. They pierced through me the same way Ben's did. I gasped, trying to catch the breath I'd been unknowingly holding.

"You okay?" He asked.

I shook it off. "I'm fine."

"You checked out for a second."

"Did I?"

"Like you saw a ghost."

How do you tell a man you have been sleeping with his son? You don't. You look deeper into those eyes and search for more. And that's what I did.

"You know earlier when you said you weren't sure another man could find you attractive again in that way?"

"Of course." I was taken aback that he remembered.

"First, you are. And second, almost every man that walked by was trying to catch your eye."

"Haha. Funny."

"Maybe what makes you so beautiful is your naivety about how truly stunning you are."

I processed what he was saying. "Maybe when the compliments stopped, you believed it was because you were no longer worthy of them," he continued.

He pulled his chair closer to me and took my hands in his. He moved his mouth towards my ear and spoke softly, "I would like to show you how worthy you are of them."

I smiled. Embarrassed a little. Strange, I thought to myself. Ben had been straightforward with me. I enjoyed it. But it didn't turn my stomach like Beau's words did.

I leaned in, taking a page from his book, and whispered in his ear. "Want to go back to my place?"

He pulled away, searching my eyes. "Your eyes sparkle. It's like they're dancing."

"So, is that a yes?" I said as I gently moved my hand along his thigh.

"Yes." He looked around until he caught our server's attention and motioned for the check.

"You had me worried I'd misread you," I admitted. I felt emboldened but unsure that I was reading his cues correctly.

"You read me like a book."

The waitress brought the bill and the two glasses of wine we ordered. He looked at them and then me. "I have wine at home," I said.

I offered to split the bill, but he laughed at that. Somehow, I knew that would not be an option, but I didn't want to be presumptuous either. This world of dating, meeting people, and hooking up was all new to me. I didn't know the social norms for this age and dating or if there were any.

We walked hand in hand back to my place. Before we walked in, he pulled me in for a long kiss. It was tender and gentle, with just enough tongue to remind me how much fun kissing was, no matter the age.

"This is it. It's small but quaint," I said as he followed me inside.

"I like what you've done with the place."

"It still has work. It's a rental. It's also really, really small. But it's starting to feel like mine." I walked to the kitchen and pulled out two glasses and a chilled bottle of wine.

"You have a wine preference?" I asked.

"I prefer all wines."

"How about a Zinfandel? All the way from California, even."

"If you had said from New Jersey, I would have questioned your taste." I laughed. I began uncorking the bottle when he walked over next to me. He put his hand on top of mine, gently coercing the opener from me, his touch lingering. "Let me," he finally said. I slowly let go of the opener, feeling his touch on my hand. I moved the glasses closer, and he began to pour.

"You have good taste in wine," he said.

"Thank you." I took the glass he handed me. "I get the sense you might be an expert."

He chuckled, then took a sip of his wine. "An expert I am not. But I've definitely educated myself on it." He took another sip and began to speak but stopped.

"What?" I asked. "This isn't good?"

"No. This is great. I was trying to think of the words to say without sounding...I don't know what the word is, but..."

"I can handle it. Whatever it is." I said, teasing him as I took another sip of my wine.

"The things we taste and enjoy are among life's great pleasures. Kind of like sex..." He paused to look at me. "Can I go there?"

"To a sex analogy? Absolutely. I'll assume it's a form of foreplay."

"I like that." He moved closer to me. I could almost feel his breath on me.

"A fine wine is like good sex when both people find pleasure together, emotionally and physically. A cheap wine leaves a bad taste, and maybe only one person gets something from it. But both usually regret that they didn't drink the finer wine. The things we taste and enjoy are among life's great pleasures."

"I'm glad this is not a cheap wine then." He takes my glass from me.

"Close your eyes. I want to show you something."

"But I can't see if my eyes are closed."

"You will. I promise."

I close my eyes. Nervous. Uneasy. But, above all, anticipating what's next.

"Trust me. This will be fun." I hear him take a sip from his glass and set it back down.

"Wait. So you get to drink, and I get to imagine you drinking? That hardly seems like a lesson in wine." He doesn't respond.

I startle as I feel his finger slowly paint its way across my lips, leaving behind a trail of wine.

"Lick your lips. Taste it there first. Can you feel it?" I licked at the trail of wine he left, his finger still sitting as if waiting for me to lick it, too. He moves it away before I can.

"Nice, right? Do you feel that? It sets a whole series of sensations in motion." I was feeling sensations. Yes. My whole body was waking up, aroused at Beau touching me so softly, purposefully. And this was only wine.

"Yes. Sensations," I said slowly, breathy.

"Now open your eyes." I did as I was told. He took another sip, this time keeping the sip in his mouth momentarily before swallowing. Slowly, he licked his lips while locking eyes with me. "Now you."

He handed me my wine as he moved even closer.

"Smell that." I did as he said. "Smell the essence of berries. The dark, jammy notes. Hints of pepper and chocolate. Now, take a small sip. He watched intently as I moved my glass to my lips, allowing me to taste a little before he slowly pulled my hand away. His eyes never left mine. I did not know wine could be so sexy.

"Can you taste the different flavors?" I swallowed. Before I could answer, I felt his lips on mine—gentle, soft, intentional. He parted my lips, allowing his tongue to find its way inside my mouth, twisting with my own tongue—just briefly. He stopped, "I can taste it. It blends perfectly with the taste in my mouth."

He took the wine glass from my hand and placed it beside his. He moved his hand to my neck underneath my hair, his thumb stroking my cheek. His other hand moved to my lips, his thumb brushing along where he had left the first taste for me.

"I want to taste you, Scarlet."

"I want you to taste me," I said in a voice that clearly said I am melting at your touch. He kissed me softly at first, our tongues slowly moving, finding their rhythm. The taste of wine was long gone, but the effect clearly lingered.

"I want to taste all of you," he said as his mouth moved down my neck. He put his finger in his wine glass, touched it to my lips, and then let his finger trail down my neck and toward the space exposed between my breasts. Then he licked slowly from my lips to my breasts. I couldn't help but gently moan. This had to be the most sensual thing a man had ever done to me. He pulled my dress over my head, dipped his finger back in the wine glass, and continued the trail. Down my stomach. Into my belly button. And then to the base of my panties. He was on his knees now. His tongue moved slowly behind the finger that was pulling my underwear off.

"God, you're beautiful." The smart ass, ruin the moment woman in me kept her mouth shut. It would have been easy to ask what part of me he meant. My crotch? Or me? But I knew he meant me. For once, I knew the compliment was meant for me. He did not reach for more wine, but his tongue continued to explore me. Slowly moving. And then his fingers found their way inside me while his tongue moved more vigorously. This was beautiful oral sex like I hadn't had in so long. Not like with Ben. Certainly not Shane. This was different. Or I was suddenly aware, feeling uninhibited to allow myself to enjoy it. I orgasmed quickly. Despite how Ben had made me feel, I still felt like I had a backlog of orgasms to make up for; I would not let myself feel any emotion other than exhilaration.

I unbuttoned Beau's pants. They dropped to the floor, allowing his excitement to be free and noticeable. I brushed my hand across him before lifting his shirt off. I liked his chest, its small spattering of hair, and the ease with which my fingers and tongue moved over it. I reached behind him for the glass of wine. I took a small sip and then dipped my finger in the glass. Making a wine trail down his chest that I licked as I drew it, finishing with a final touch on his eagerly waiting appendage. I tasted him, and he enthusiastically responded with moans of pleasure. He was manscaped, and tasting him was wonderful without the fear of pubic hair. He pulled me up before he allowed himself to orgasm. He kissed me hard.

"I want to be inside of you," he said as he kissed my neck. I grabbed his hand as I walked past him to the bedroom.

"Do you have a favorite way?" I asked playfully.

"All of them." He said, making me laugh.

"Do you?" He asked.

"On top," I said emphatically.

"I can do that."

We spent the next hour discovering each other in bed.

We'd stop and talk briefly, then he'd find his way inside of me again. It was fluid and easy with him. We dozed off in each other's arms, not waking until the morning.

I woke first. I watched him briefly as he slept on his side next to me. I got out of bed, put on a T-shirt and some clean underwear, and headed to the kitchen to make coffee. I walked back to the bedroom, handing him his cup of coffee. He smiled at me as he sat up in the bed, pulling the sheets up to cover his naked lower half.

"Good morning," he said.

"Good morning back. I assume you drink this." He took it from me.

"Addicted. Actually."

"Me, too. Can't start my day without it. Didn't know if you put anything in it."

"Nope. Black is perfect." He took a sip. "Oh, this is good."

"Pushed a button. Can't take much credit." He laughed.

"Last night was fun," he said.

"It was. You were impressive."

"Likewise."

"You know it dawned on me this morning while I patiently waited for both our coffees to brew that neither of us asked about a condom."

"Oh shit. You're right. God, it's been so long, and..."

"No. I get it. Then I thought, there are so many other things."

"Like?"

"Like, do you need Viagra?"

"I'm not sure if I should be insulted or flattered."

I laughed at my own candor. "Honestly, I was suddenly hit with this thought of what if I have to call an ambulance and they ask me what kind of medications you're on. Because let's face it, there's a good chance either of us is on something."

"I'm not."

"Really? Oh good. I'm not either."

"Well, we are clearly the exceptions to the rule then." We both laughed. He reached for my hand, careful not to spill any of his coffee. "I like that you're thinking of these things. This means last night was more than just a one-night stand. At least, I hope that's what that means."

"No other medical things I need to know about first? God, that sounds like we're old."

"We aren't old. Just mature. And no. You saw me swim. I think I proved I can keep up."

"Well, then, I think we can at least make it more than one night." We both moved in for a kiss.

"I like you," he said.

"Ditto."

TWELVE

FOR THE NEXT WEEK, we became routine. We'd meet for a quiet dinner and drinks and then return to my place, where the sex was amazing. He always stayed the night and didn't leave until the morning. I was discovering a level of intimacy with him both emotionally and physically that I hadn't had with Shane and certainly not with Ben.

Beau's hands touched me differently. I loved how he moved them from my shoulders alongside my breasts and the curves of my hips. How his lips moved from mine to my neck, lingering on my breasts, my belly button, before his arms wrapped around my legs and drew me in tighter for him to explore me.

I liked that he would change his cadence, sometimes fast, sometimes so slow and purposeful. And his fingers moved inside me at just the right moment. I felt selfish in those moments. The only thing I could give back was my moans of satisfaction. And then asking him to be inside me so we could both share the pleasure. He smiled at me when I asked, taking one more pass with his tongue before pulling me to the edge of the bed and entering me slowly. Several times like that. And then I knew when his patience was tested because he began to move quickly. His eyes closed as he came inside me. Apologizing. For nothing, I thought. That I could still make a man lose himself that quickly was empowering. He would fall to my side, moving my hair behind my ear, kissing my neck as I felt his fingers rubbing me until I, too, lost control of myself. As my back arched in pleasure, I felt a nibble on my breasts and a gentle sucking that reminded me other parts of my body were capable of pleasure too.

It was easy to let myself be unencumbered with Beau. He was a tender and sweet lover. He took his time with me. He was never in a hurry. At first, I wondered if it was because he needed more time to get aroused, given his age. He did not.

I didn't know his sexual history. I tried not to ask too many questions. I wasn't sure where my current situation was going to take me. So far, I liked it here. I enjoyed this slower pace of living and of being with Beau. I suppose, despite the fear of getting old faster than I was ready, I wanted to enjoy this time of discovery.

It felt so different than when I was young. Geez, really, if I thought about it, I stopped dating in my early twenties. I was married by twenty-five and devoted to one man, Shane, for the next thirty years.

Until Carter. Of course, Carter was the wake-up call I had avoided for so long. While a messy situation, he was an indirect, unintended messenger of all the things I had been avoiding or, at a minimum, unwilling to acknowledge.

But Beau was new in an old kind of way. I did not look around the world and see sexy, exciting men in their fifties and sixties. They scared me, to be honest. They weren't packaged like they used to be. But who was I to judge them, really? I wasn't packaged the same anymore either. Plump boobs became mom boobs became lifeless hanging wonders found midway down my torso. If it weren't for the joy I saw Ben take in them, and now Beau, I would have said no man would find them pleasing. But they did, which made me understand the human body is so much more than looking like perfection. It's still capable of eliciting a sexual response and undoubtedly capable of feeling it as well.

Beau and I spent hours talking before sex and after sex. The excitement of having sex with someone new again was punctuated by deep, meaningful conversations about life, love, marriage, and family. I felt comfortable opening up to him. I loved that about this age. There were no false pretenses. We didn't have to be anything but our true, authentic selves. A small part of me recognized that I could fall in love with this man. It was unexpected. It was scary. But it was also exciting and fun and so easy with Beau.

We often found ourselves sitting out looking over the ocean in the morning. It was peaceful. We'd each drink two Nespressos before deciding we needed to eat something. On this particular morning, I returned with our second cup.

"You know, having a coffee maker would be more cost-efficient."

"Before you, it wasn't," I winked at him as I said it. "Life's short. It's one of those little things I afford myself even if I know I don't have a ton of excess to splurge."

He laughed under his breath. "You know, my ex once accused me of having a bank account in the Caymans. She thought I was hiding money from her. I was a fucking firefighter." I almost spit up my coffee.

Jokingly, I asked, "Well, did you?"

"God, no. She tried so hard to find so many things wrong with me. She accused me of so many things even before we started the divorce process. I just got so tired of always being a bad guy. I guess that's when I realized I didn't want to fight anymore."

"That's hard. I get it."

"Was it the same for you?" he asked.

"No. It was more like he was completely disconnected from me. And somewhere along the way, I stopped loving him for him and realized I only really loved him as the father of my children. Which is beautiful. Yes. And he would always be that man to me. But I needed more. I needed him to be his own person. More than anything, I needed us to be connected. And that was totally severed."

"Was he surprised?" I'd never talked with another man about my divorce. It provided a different perspective, and I appreciated the opportunity to share and be heard.

"Yes and no. I had an emotional affair..." I looked at him to see how he'd react. He kept watching me intently. No eye roll. No judgment. "And I told him. At first, I think it scared him and he said he wanted to work it out. But we couldn't. And, honestly, I couldn't. I wouldn't have opened up to someone else if our marriage had even a little hope. I knew I couldn't be happy. And I knew it would hang over us if we stayed together."

"Wow. That's deep."

"Yours wasn't?"

"I don't know. It was a long time coming, too. Our kids saw it. She was angry all the time. But I'm not sure she even knew why she was angry. It was exhausting. I was relieved when we finally agreed to get divorced." His honesty made him even more endearing.

"I never cried when we got divorced, and I never cried when it ended. It was like this floodgate was opened, but it wasn't water that needed to be drained. Instead, I felt relief—like you. And it felt good. Scary, but good. You think that makes me heartless?" I asked.

Crying I could do at the drop of a hat. Two seconds into a Hallmark commercial, I know I'll be unable to speak. I watch an inspirational athletic moment. Hear a story of overcoming the odds. I cry. My own marriage ending did not evoke that emotion. I wondered if I was normal. Or if my situation was simply that I was the one who strayed; I was the one who burned my marriage's bridge.

"No. It makes you human. Do you think he cried?" He asked.

"Hardly. That's not the kind of man he is."

"I don't think most men are. At least not the ones I know."

"Did you cry?" I was curious.

"I was sad. I felt like I failed. But no."

I didn't know how to ask. Did he cheat like me? Was he wearing a scarlet letter, too?

"Were you unfaithful?"

"She thinks so. I'm unsure where that line got muddied anymore, and she couldn't hear my words. But that was always the problem. She didn't want to hear my words. And she didn't want to believe them anyway. I didn't want to go the rest of my life defending myself from something I never did."

We sat there quietly for a moment, digesting our words. I never regretted being married to Shane. I loved the life I had with him. I wondered if Beau had felt the same way about his life.

"Would you do it differently if you could?' I wondered.

"I don't think so. Mostly because my kids are pretty amazing. You?"

"I've thought about it a lot. I wouldn't change my life or the people I got to love along the way. They allowed me to become who I am today. I needed them to find my way here," I explained.

"So, you never believed in one happily ever after?"

"I don't think so. I don't know if I ever looked at anyone and thought they were supposed to be my happily ever after. It took me a really long time to realize I was my own happily ever after. I would consider myself extra lucky if someone was by my side." I looked at him as he watched me. I could see him processing what my words might have meant in the context of his own life.

"I like that," he said.

"I've learned to be nicer to the memories of love's past. All of them. Even the ones that made me cringe in hindsight." We both laughed at that. "They all had their place."

"The marriage is the hardest part, though. At least for me," he offered.

"Marriage is a contract. Not a love letter. We think we got it all figured out in our twenties. We skip happily along until we get tripped up by objects we don't see coming. Shit, sometimes we even get in our own way."

"Sometimes? Hah." I laughed at his revelation. "I like your perspective of letting bitterness dissolve away."

"You think you'd ever get married again?" I wondered.

"I don't know. Probably not. You?"

"I like marriage. I liked being married. Sometimes, things just end. But marriage is still beautiful."

"I like how easy it is to talk with you. It's so refreshing." Even his segways from potentially uncomfortable topics were pleasant.

"Must be my Cali charm."

"Or that you're above the pretense and bullshit."

"Or that."

LATER THAT DAY, I met Missy for lunch. I was nervous, wondering if the connection we had made at book club was only in the moment or if we had made a genuine connection. My overactive imagination questioned if she had been sent by Abby and her minions to gather dirt on the new woman in town. My world had become a crazy place of lust. I was bursting at the seams to talk to another woman about the unexpected turns my life had taken since I arrived here. I really needed a friend. I didn't know if I could tell her everything, but I needed to tell someone something.

My fears were immediately laid to rest when she saw me walk in, scurrying over to me, barely containing her excitement and hugged me. "Oh my god, I have been dying to talk with you." Had she seen me out with Beau? I never thought of looking around and seeing if I knew anyone. I just figured I didn't.

"I hope not to share mean divorced women's book club gossip about me?" I said, half joking.

"Oh, God, no. Those women are the gossip. Not you." A sense of relief came over me.

The waiter came over with water for us. Missy looked at me. "You want a drink, right? I mean, it's not too early to drink something." She made me laugh.

"I'd like a Pornstar Martini," she said. "Have you had one before?" I shook my head no. She made a two sign to the waiter, and he walked off. "Best drink you'll ever have. I had one in Curacao a few years ago, and there's no return from that one."

The waiter brought our drinks. I poured the prosecco into the martini glass and watched it turn a beautiful shade of orange as it mixed with the vanilla vodka and passion fruit juice. Missy looked up at me with a big smile on her face. "Magic." She raised her glass. "Here's to making new friends."

"Cheers," I said as we carefully clinked our very full martini glasses. One sip and I was also hooked. We both ordered a salad and munched on bread slices while we waited for food.

Missy was a talker. I liked that. She seemed different from the other women.

"Are you from here?" I asked, wondering if she was from somewhere else and if she related to being an outlier like I was.

"I grew up here. Went to USC. Did the Greek life thing. Met a man. Married way too young. Had kids way too young. We moved back here. I got bored." She paused, took an extra long sip of her drink, looked at me, and continued speaking. "The kids went off to college. And I went and found myself..."

"That sounds like a good thing," I offered.

"I found myself a fling," she said quietly under her breath, then took another big sip. My drink hit me quickly and I had half of what she did. I was happy when the waiter brought our food out. I quickly had a few bites, hoping it would act to absorb the alcohol.

"Oh my. I've never told anyone that before." She was on a roll, spilling her story. "I mean, the whole fucking town knows. But I've never actually said it to anyone before."

"It's a small town. You had to figure."

"Maybe I did it on purpose. If Cal found out, he'd leave me. It'd be so easy."

"Obviously, he did."

"Hah. That and some. That son of a bitch couldn't stand that I would do that to him, forget all the other shit in our marriage. He went and propositioned my best friend. Told her I was a cheat. That he loved me. Couldn't bear to lose me. Then fucked her brains out."

My mouth dropped. And then a lightbulb clicked. "Margo?"

"Damn. You're good."

"Oh, that sucks, Missy."

"It's been a lot of years. I wanted out. He just made it a million times easier."

"And the man you...you..."

"Cheated with?" I nodded. "He was literally that. It was fun. It was not emotional. It was like you said at book club: it was sex without the intimacy. It ended after a couple of months. He was a nice guy."

"His name wasn't Beau, was it?" She chuckled when I asked.

"Beau Sanders?" I didn't know Beau or Ben's last name. "Hah. Abby would have killed me."

"They've been divorced a long time." I wanted to put my hand over my mouth as soon as I said it.

"Oh, girl. You've met Beau?"

"Maybe."

"Oh, go on. I gotta hear this."

"Nothing to tell. He seemed like a very nice man, that's all," I said.

"He's a catch, girlfriend. The best thing he ever did was leave Abby. Not sure why he hasn't found anyone since."

"Small town, I'm guessing." She polished off her Pornstar martini and gave me a questioning look. "God, no. That thing is potent," I quickly responded.

"Yeah. You're right. I probably just scared the shit out of you with my confessional. You just feel like a sister in arms. And I could seriously use a sister in arms."

"Then you've found the right person."

We finished our lunch. I shared the parts of my story that were relevant to my being on Sullivan's Island. I did not tell her about Ben or elaborate about Beau. It was nice to talk freely to another woman who understood what it was like to be the bad person in a marriage ending.

"We don't always have to be the victim when something goes sideways in a marriage," I said.

"No kidding. But that's what everyone around here thinks. You become branded."

"I call it wearing my scarlet letter. A big fat D."

"Oooh, I see what you did there." With that, I had just made a new friend who could relate and not judge me. We shared the letter D. Scarlet was uniquely mine.

"We could be a secret society," she said, laughing.

"I think the whole point of wearing the scarlet letter is so everyone knows you wronged."

She thought about it and then let it go. "I can't wait to do this again, my sister in arms."

THIRTEEN

THAT NIGHT, I told Beau about Missy. Thankfully, he had no reservations about my new friend. He knew her ex, Cal, and had nothing to say about him. "Are you always this neutral?" I asked.

"Only when it's none of my business. Too many busy bodies in a small town as it is."

"Fair enough. I'm glad you don't hate her. I need a friend."

He ran his finger along the edge of my shirt collar, then played with my collarbone, dipping his thumb in the shallow pool my skin created behind the bone. "I'm your friend."

"With benefits. I know."

"I like this spot," he said as he kissed along my collarbone, gently following the line to my shoulder. He carefully pulled my shirt sleeve down to expose more skin. I loved his lips as they moved along my shoulder. He tugged at my shirt when it would go no farther. Looking up at me, he said, "This is in my way."

146

I tugged at my shirt. "This?" His eyes said *yes*. "I can take care of that." I took my time, finding joy in his impatience. I got up from the couch and turned away from him. I pulled my shirt off and then began taking off my jean shorts. My body silhouetted in the evening light, I let him take me in. "I don't think you have a bad side," he said as he came in from behind. His clothes were discarded in a pile next to my shorts. I could feel him hard against me. His hand reached around my front and slid down my belly and into my black lacy underwear. His other hand managed to unclasp the back of my matching black lacy bra. Without looking back, without confirmation this was how he wanted it, I kneeled on the couch. He was quick to enter, quicker to finish. It made me giggle. "God, what is it about you? I've lost all control."

I turned around to face him, lying down on the couch. "That's okay. My turn now." His eyes twinkled as he reached down, bringing me to climax quickly.

"God, what is it about you?" I held in my laugh as I said it. "I've lost all control."

I LOVED FALLING asleep next to Beau. He always grabbed my hand, wrapping his fingers gently through mine. I loved feeling his breath on my neck in the mornings as he nuzzled in closely. Some mornings, he'd start with a simple "Good morning." And then he'd roll on top of me, eager to be inside me again. I didn't tire of it. I hoped it would go on for a long time. I had become very fond of Beau.

"When do you think couples stop having sex?" I asked him.

"God, I hope never." I laughed, imagining an eager octogenarian still pleasing his partner.

I never bought the narrative that sex has to wane with age. Maybe it goes dormant for those years when listening to your body tell you it needs to be touched is not something that could always just happen. Life made us disinterested, maybe, or it said *I'm exhausted,* or *I feel like shit.* And yes, I can do it myself with much less effort. Default mode.

For some women, the sex stops. That wasn't my case with Shane. We had sex for sex's sake. It wasn't intimate, though. I would ask myself what that meant sometimes. Was I expecting too much? Is this just the course of things over time? But I knew it wasn't. It felt empty. There was a void. And as much as Shane was able to satisfy the physical part of my needs, I knew someday it wouldn't be about sex anymore. We were getting older. While I wanted to believe that I would be that woman having sex into her seventies, I knew an emotional connection would be equally, if not more, satisfying as we got older.

Carter reminded me of that. He reminded me how I could feel whole by a man's words. Not just the words that told me I was beautiful. But the ones that said we had a deeper understanding of one another. That's what Carter did for me.

Carter's beautiful sext messages enlightened me about a man's wants. Or at least his desires. He was honest with me. Shane would blow me off if I asked what he wanted or needed in the bedroom. To him, it was "fine the way it is." A frustrating yet typical response to my efforts to deepen our connection. Carter once said every man wants to wake up to a blow job. I did not get to do that to him. I imagined over and over how I would do it. How it would turn him on. How I wouldn't let him be inside me; that I fully wanted to satisfy him first thing in the morning.

I told him I wanted him to move in behind me while I was sleeping, begin touching me... and then, when I was wet and ready, he should slide inside me from behind. I told him that. I wanted those things with him. I could never share that with Shane.

And those thoughts were buried until Beau. The physical and emotional intimacy with Beau was on a different level. And while we hadn't talked about fantasies or particular ways to please each other, he seemed to know. More than once in those first weeks, I awoke with Beau hard against my back, touching me gently, kissing my neck, slowly waking me, all the different parts of me, as he moved down my body with his mouth and his hands. It was more than I had imagined as I felt him slide inside me slowly from behind.

On other mornings, I would do the waking testing Carter's proclamation of a morning blow job, finding it quickly validated. Damn you, Carter, I thought as Beau came in my mouth. Damning Carter's still occasional haunting of my thoughts, I was grateful to have dodged that bullet with him. And thankful that he shared with me things that had been repressed in my repertoire of sexual tricks.

Beau and I would talk naked over coffee in bed after we'd had sex about how unexpected and different it was to be in a relationship at this age. There were no pretenses. We were both uninhibited. I let myself begin to fall in love with him. I gave all of myself when I didn't know I could anymore. And he gave them to me. To say we don't or can't evolve as lovers as we age is a fallacy. We take all the learnings, all the trials and errors of earlier lives, loves, and marriages, and form a basis to understand the kind of person we are and to know the type of person we want to be with in the end. To know I could still drive a man to want me was a beautiful result of giving in – and letting go – of those inhibitions. We evolve. Beau has taught me to evolve. We had become the other's evolution in a world of stagnant progress.

FOURTEEN

THE DAY BEFORE EMILY ARRIVED, I got a text from an unknown number. It was Carter. I had removed him from my contacts, but he did not do the same. Beyond the "Hi, it's Carter" that popped up on my home screen, I did not read it. I was enjoying my new life. Carter had turned my world upside down. But he was also what I needed to finally see things more clearly in my marriage to Shane. I had been hovering in a state of purgatory for so long. Carter may not have been a brave move for me. Maybe even cowardly connecting with a married man. Stupid perhaps. But as time passed, I no longer considered Carter a missed opportunity. In those moments when we were filling emotional voids for each other, my vision was undoubtedly blurred. My vision was clear now. I was admittedly falling in love with Beau. The novelty that was Carter no longer existent.

His second text came in shortly before Emily arrived. I didn't open that one, either. I had no desire to hear what he had to say. I hoped my silent nonresponse would be enough for him to stop reaching out. While I knew Carter and I were wrong and would never be, he had hurt me. I was moving my life forward, not lamenting lost opportunities from a lifetime ago. And certainly not the lost opportunity of the last year.

Thankfully, Emily bounded in the front door before I could overthink anything. Any and all thoughts of Carter left me at that moment. I had my Emily for a few days, and my heart exploded. It also meant no more sleepovers with Beau. "Pent-up desire is a good thing," he said as I shared about Emily.

"Can I meet her?" he asked as he walked out the door.

"Really? That's kind of a big deal, don't you think?" I asked, secretly excited he offered.

"Life's short, Scar. Pretty sure I'm falling in love with you, so..." He put his hands up in the what- do-we-have-to-lose shrug? And turned to leave. I was speechless. He smiled, "Cat got your tongue?"

He knew it did.

"Ditto," I managed. His smile growing. "I want to try High Thyme. Sevenish."

"Great choice. Can't wait to meet Emily." He blew me a kiss and walked to his car.

Emily and I spent the day exploring my surrounding neighborhood on foot. We walked down Middle Street, saw High Thyme, and were both excited about our dinner.

"Did I tell you Beau will be there?"

"No. But you have so much to tell me about Beau, Mom."

"You have to tell me if it gets weird for you, though. It can't be easy having your mom talk about another man."

"I just want you to be happy. You seem happy. You just don't have to give me intimate details," she said.

"Oh, but the sex is the best part."

"Oh my god, Mom. No." We both laughed. On that note, we headed home to get ready for dinner with Beau. Knowing I wouldn't be alone with him later, I was still excited to see him. Emily said I looked happy, and he was a huge reason my face hurt from constantly smiling.

I popped open a bottle of prosecco as we took our time readying for dinner. Prosecco had always been a gateway to conversation for us. When Emily came home from college with her friends in tow, we'd sit around the table, eating crackers and cheese while drinking prosecco. She and her friends had not quite mastered wine at that point, preferring the bubbles and mild sweetness of prosecco. I had learned to let the prosecco do the talking and mostly be a fly on a wall while they gossiped and overshared about their college life. I wanted to cringe at times. Other times, I welcomed their questions about my own experiences. I liked to think I was the cool mom.

During one of our more detailed sexual prosecco-fueled conversations, Emily and her two roommates asked how they were supposed to know if they really orgasmed or not. I admitted my own path to learning was a process. Her friends were considerably more open to hearing my reply than Emily. I was discreet in my answer. I missed the sexual revolution of the sixties, I confessed.

"Orgasms were talked about like they were so easy to come by," I said. It drew a collective moan from the girls.

"Haha, Mom. No pun there," Emily snarked.

"Seriously, it's a process. And it's easier for some than others. Just be open to figuring it out." The next day, I ordered three vibrators and had them shipped to their apartment back at college.

I heard Emily happily humming as she readied for our night out, making me smile.

"I miss having you around, Em," I said.

"I miss you, too. But I haven't been around since I was like eighteen."

"I know. I was just thinking about all our prosecco conversations."

"Oh, God. Those could be awkward sometimes."

"I thought they were fun," I confessed. "I got a little extra glimpse into your world."

"Sometimes too much, if I recall." It was just the right amount, I thought. I knew she was experiencing life and doing things as I hoped she would.

"You never thanked me for sending you, Cami, and Annie those vibrators. I never asked, but I'm assuming you figured it out."

I heard a gag. Emily walked out of the bathroom, her hair done, her makeup on, and her empty glass waving in the air.

"There are some things, Mother, that I will not share with you." She filled her empty glass and then mine. "But, let's just say they were all well received." We both giggled.

EMILY and I sat at our table inside the restaurant. The outside was loud and full of excited tourists. I knew I was only one tier above being a tourist. I wouldn't be considered a local yet. But I liked it here.

We sat in a perfect, secluded corner. I was excited for her to meet Beau. I knew Emily wouldn't compare Beau to Shane or be uninterested. He was easy to talk to, and she could speak nonstop if she wanted. I didn't expect their meeting to be anything but pleasant.

We ordered drinks while we waited. He texted that he would be a few minutes late but that he had a surprise for us. I wondered what kind of surprise he would be bringing Emily, whom he'd never met, and me. Beyond bringing a bottle of wine on occasion, we weren't at the gift-giving stage yet.

I kept my eye on the front entrance. It was busy, and people were constantly walking in and out. I looked up and was stunned when I saw Carter enter the door. I could feel my temperature rise when I spotted him across the room. Here. Now. God, was this why he was texting me? I pulled out my phone and quickly read the two texts: "Hi, It's Carter. Not what you expected, I know. But I really need to see you." Followed by: "Hey, I'm in town. Can we please meet?"

"Oh, fuck," I said under my breath.

"You okay, Mom?" Emily asked.

I didn't want him to see me, but it was too late. He started to walk over, and I shook my head, "No."

"I'm fine. I just need to use the bathroom." I excused myself from the table, trying to sneak around people so he wouldn't continue coming my way. I covered my face with my purse as I headed toward the bathroom. I needed a quiet space to think. I needed to get there before he got to me. I could see him pursuing me. Thankfully, he did not call out to me.

I quickly closed the door behind me, putting my back against it, feeling myself need to breathe. I took in two big breaths. My mind was spinning. Damn him. He said he couldn't do it to his wife and family. I respected that. Why couldn't he respect my need to move forward and start new? It had been nearly a year since I cut him off. I didn't give him hope.

There was a knock on the door. I heard him say my name. I took another deep breath and ripped open the door.

"What the fuck, Carter? I'm starting over."

"Just let me explain."

"Explain what? You already did that. And I moved on from it."

"I didn't." He looked sad. We stood in the hallway between the men's and women's restrooms.

"Jesus, not here." We walked out the back door I noticed the employees had been using. I did not want to have to explain any of this to Emily or Beau.

"What, Carter? What?" My tone was angry. And annoyance.

"I love you, Scar. I really do." He reached for my arm, but I swatted it away.

"You don't love me. You love the idea of me."

"There's no difference. They both involve loving you." I softened my stance.

"We got caught up. I was excited. You were exciting. We were an unknown, unanswered question. We were going off some memories from when we were young. When it was safe. But you don't know me now. I don't know you. Ours was sexual tension when we were both lonely."

"I didn't know I was lonely until you." I wanted to laugh at that.

"Maybe. But if you want to leave your marriage, you have to decide that. I will not be a catalyst. I have moved on. I am not what you want."

"But you are. You're all I think about." I was getting frustrated at his inability to grasp what I was saying.

"You think about me now. But what happens down the road when you realize that your kids should have come first?"

"They have their mom." I rolled my eyes.

"At first. Then you'll miss them and resent me because somehow I didn't meet the expectations your fantasy created. I don't want to be resented. I want to live my life on my terms and not worry about breaking anyone else doing it."

"I'm in love with you, Scar. I can't resent you." The reality was that if I explored a future with Carter, I would always feel the shadow of guilt present and the potential for resentment to grow deep.

Carter was the one man I thought I would do anything for. I wanted him desperately during our short dalliance. He made me feel like a woman again. I had completely let him go over the last many months. Carter walking back into my life now was unexpected. I had left California. I did not tell him where I was going. I liked knowing the prospect of our paths ever crossing again was non-existent. There would be no chance encounters here. I had moved on. I didn't want to know how he found me. It didn't matter. It was bold of him to assume I would be open to conversation.

"Carter, I was never in love with you. The idea, maybe. You were my out. And it turns out the idea you existed was enough. I was a game to you. You were never leaving."

"I'll admit, at first, maybe. I liked the effect I had on you. But you had the same effect on me."

My world collided with Carter's at precisely the right time to discover we were both unhappy in our marriages. It felt serendipitous as if we were meant to explore each other and help one another figure out our respective places. Those chance texts and honest words fueled by emotional voids were how I imagine most affairs began in the first place.

"Carter, I'm sorry that things aren't better for you. But please, if you really cared for me, even loved me, you would be happy for me. I am loving this new life I'm leading. It's fresh. I needed a new beginning, and I'm finding it here. Please, understand that."

He leaned against the wall, briefly closing his eyes, then spoke. "I do. I really do. I guess I just needed to know there was no chance. But also that you're good. And that you're happy. That's all I want for you. Honestly." Carter hugged me tightly. "I'm glad you're happy," he whispered in my ear. He pulled away from me and walked towards the parking lot. I saw him wipe his face. The moisture from that tear on my cheek.

Carter walking back into my life was not what I expected. I was happy in my new beginning. I was already trying to balance emotions, teetering precariously on the brink of collapse as I tried to figure out love with Beau and how to handle things with Ben when he returned.

I collected myself. Carter had been decent and left without a scene. I was happy about that. A weight had been lifted, I thought. When I walked back, I was stunned to find Ben sitting at the table with Emily and Beau. One weight lifted, a heavier one staring at me head-on. My eyes met Ben's, and he shook his head, acknowledging that he would not make this awkward. Such maturity for his age.

Beau got up as I approached and kissed me on the cheek. I sat down next to him.

"You okay? You look like you've seen a ghost." Emily asked. Two, I thought.

"Nope. All's good." I looked at Ben. He stood up to shake my hand.

"This is my son, Ben," Beau said, unknowingly reintroducing us.

"I hope you don't mind. Ben just got back this afternoon. He stopped by my place, and I thought it'd be a perfect time for him to meet you and, of course, Emily," Beau said, beaming.

"You're back early," I said.

"You two know each other?" Beau asked. I felt like a deer in the headlights.

"No. I'm sure you've told her I was in the Navy. Have been gone for a few days." Ben was picking up the slack.

"Yes, yes, you did." I looked at Beau hoping he'd bought my awful performance. "And you've met Emily? I'm sorry I wasn't here to introduce you."

"She's exactly as you described. Maybe even prettier in person," Beau said. I think she might have blushed. But I couldn't tell if it was because of the cliché compliment or that she had Ben sitting next to her.

Emily had her fair share of boyfriends over the years. None of them were ever worthy of more than that. She wasn't eager to get married or start a family. I had rarely seen her gush over any of them. But, sitting next to Ben, she was obviously quite smitten. I was relieved to see the two of them carry on a conversation amongst themselves, involving Beau and me on a minimal level.

"They have good chemistry," Beau whispered as his hand rubbed my leg.

"He seems like a nice enough man."

"I mean, he is my son." I smiled at Beau, studied his face, and felt a sense of calm come over me. This man was falling in love with me. He made me laugh and smile. He made me feel whole when parts of me felt broken. Surely, he wouldn't hate me if he ever discovered that Ben and I had a fling before him. There's been nothing since. And watching Ben with Emily confirmed my belief that Ben and someone younger made way more sense than Ben and a cougar.

Dinner was lovely. Ben asked if Emily wanted to join him for drinks at Poe's. She looked at me, then back at Ben. I answered for her, "Of course she does. Just get her home safely." She smiled as she grabbed her purse from the seat.

We walked out together. Emily and Beau both stopped at the restroom. For the first time, it felt slightly awkward between me and Ben. "I didn't know," I offered.

"How could you?" He whispered in my ear, "We'll talk later. It doesn't have to be weird."

Emily returned, and she and Ben headed out for drinks. I stood there waiting for Beau's return, thinking *this could not be any weirder*.

FIFTEEN

EMILY WALKED in shortly before midnight. Mom mode kicked in, and I did not fall asleep until I heard her back in the house. I imagine I was equally worried that Ben might slip up and tell her something about me. Or, worse, I thought, they might have sex. God, what if we were Eskimo sisters?

The girls would joke about it when two of them would sleep with the same guy over the course of their college years. That likely happened somewhat frequently. The fact it had a name was amusing at the time. I couldn't remember sharing a college fling with any of my friends. But now, I might be sharing a fling with my own daughter. I did not want to be her Eskimo sister. That thought kept me tossing and turning long after she had returned.

I awoke to the sound of Emily making coffee. I wasn't sure I was ready to hear about her night with Ben. She didn't allow me to belabor my thoughts as she walked into my room carrying two cups of coffee.

"Good morning, sleepy head," she mocked. I sat up and took the coffee from her.

"This is nice. Thanks." She sat on the edge of the bed. "So, how was your night?" I asked.

"He's so hot, right? I mean, gross, asking you. But he's seriously hot." *Yes, he is.*

"You two had a nice time?"

"Yeah, we got drinks at that Poe's bar. I guess everyone hangs out there. You been? It's cool."

"I've been once. But it was lunch."

"Anyway, we had a lot to talk about. He's kind of old, honestly. And he's done a lot." There was that gut guilt feeling I had for not knowing more about Ben. "We talked about the whole divorce thing too. It was nice to have a sounding board. He was totally cool."

I wanted to ask if they kissed or if they went back to his place (*where was that anyway?*) and had sex. It would have been fine if that happened, but I had hoped not. I did not know how well I would handle being Emily's Eskimo sister.

"I'm glad you liked him." That was all I had.

"I mean, you talk about a respectful guy. He didn't even try to kiss me. And I would have let him." I felt my body relax. "You think there's something wrong with me? I mean, the women in this town aren't exactly drop-dead gorgeous and, hello, me." She jokingly pointed to herself.

"Maybe he just appreciated that his dad and your mom are in a relationship."

She thought about it for a moment. "Yeah, that would be kind of weird. Besides, I'm leaving today anyway."

"It's only been two days."

"And two nights. I decided I wanted to stop in Nashville on my way back. I got a super cheap flight. Remember Dewey from college?" I shook my head no. "Well, he got a gig off-Broadway, but it's still a gig, and a few of us will meet there to support him. It'll be fun. And I'll be back to Phoenix to figure out what the hell I want to do with my life in no time."

I was sad she wasn't staying longer. I liked our relationship as adults. And it was easier now that I was divorced. I didn't worry that I might say something that Shane did not approve of or agree with. He thought I encouraged her to take unnecessary risks and not think things through. Maybe. But I argued it was better than missing opportunities because she weighed the pros and cons until the opportunity was lost. There was a middle ground somewhere, I'm sure.

"Oh, and Ben said he would be by to say goodbye. I think he liked me regardless of the whole thing about our parents dating each other."

"No doubt he did," I assured her.

With limited time before she had to catch her flight from Charlotte to Nashville, we made the most of our day. We explored a local antique shop before getting a light lunch. We lay on the beach, read books, and played in the waves. We got iced lattes. There was no more conversation about Ben. She didn't ask more about Beau.

And she didn't mention Shane. We talked only briefly about Henry's new girlfriend. "She's super nerdy like him," she said. "But she was cool. I'm sure he'll bring her when he has a break."

"I'm glad the two of you are staying in touch. It makes me feel good knowing you have stayed connected."

"We're twins, Mom. We'll always be connected even if we're night and day."

"You might be more alike than you realize."

"Maybe. But unlikely." At least she was open to that possibility, I thought.

I planned to take her to the airport, but she informed me she had already ordered a ride.

"You didn't have to do that."

"I know. But I didn't want you to have to drive back here all by yourself. Besides, I'm sure you're eager to see Beau again." I smiled at her. "You seem really happy with him, Mom. I'm glad. You deserve someone who makes you smile on the inside and out."

Ben arrived at the same time as her ride. "Well, that was good timing," he said. He gave her a big hug. "It was fun getting to know you. If Beau and Scarlet stay a thing, I'm sure we'll see each other again."

Emily put her bag in the back of the car. She gave me a big hug. "I love you, Mom."

"I love you more, Em. Be safe. Let me know when you get to Nashville."

Ben and I stood side by side as Emily drove off. Ben, my boy toy who initially filled a sexual void before leaving on his work trip, stood next to me. I did not feel the same pull to him that I once did. I was navigating the deeper emotions associated with falling in love with his dad.

He turned to me once she was out of sight. "Inside?"

"I don't think that's a good idea."

"It's fine, Scar. I promise. I love my dad too much." I turned and led the way into the house. He sat on the couch, and I stood at the kitchen counter. I felt stronger with distance.

"How does this work, Ben?" My mind was racing, thinking quickly, talking faster. I answered my own question. "It can't. No one can know about this. I'm already wearing a scarlet letter."

He looked blankly at me. "God, that's probably a banned book here."

"No. I know. You're not an adulterer." He got up to walk towards me.

"Stay," I barked. "Sorry. This is just a lot. It's the D. And maybe now a P or M." He laughed. He was smart.

"You are not a pedophile. You did not molest me. I seduced you."

"Yes, you did. But you should have had a warning label with your age."

"God, Scar, I may be younger, but you and I both know I'm old enough to know better. I wanted you. So bad." He points to his pants. "I'm getting hard thinking about you. I think you are so fucking sexy. It's hard not to want you."

166

"Don't, please. Your dad is unexpected. Probably even more so than you. You were fun. So much fun," I admitted. I'm pretty sure I could have continued having sex with him until he'd had enough of me. But I had fallen hard for his dad.

"My dad is cool. And there is no one I'd rather see happy than him. He deserves it. If not just for putting up with the shit my mom dished out." I let him grab my hand this time when he reached for it. He kissed it softly. "I wish we could have one more time…"

"No." I stopped him.

"You didn't let me finish." I rolled my eyes in a token gesture for him to continue. "I wish we could have one more time because you are so much more than a number. But I think my dad gets that, too. I mean, after all, the apple doesn't fall far." That made me laugh. "You know, that makes you two Eskimo brothers."

He thought about it, processing it, and then the light in his head went off. "I promise he'll never know."

"Go home, Ben. And thank you for not telling anyone about us."

"Of course. It was way more fun this way. I'll miss you, Scar."

I smiled as I watched him leave my house like we had never happened. My boy toy no more.

SIXTEEN

"YOU READY?" Missy screeched as she picked me up for book club. I couldn't believe I was going back.

"No," I lamented as I hopped in her car. "But I'm glad they keep picking books I've read."

Book club was the first and third Thursday night of every month. It seemed a bit frequent to me. I wasn't the fastest reader. As with many book clubs, I believed it was more about the camaraderie between the readers than an actual deep dive into the subject matter. As a group of divorced women, I had hoped we would bond over our mutual experiences, how what we read resonated with us beyond the author's intentions, and, ultimately, to support each other in life's next chapter. After the first book club, I wasn't sure these women would be open to sharing those thoughts and feelings as much as an opportunity to condemn. I had also hoped there would be books not about divorce, cheating, or second-chance romance, all topics that seemed prevalent on our summer reading list. Rehashing our emotional trauma felt like it might get exhausting.

"Not that I'm complaining, but has the group ever read historical fiction or mystery or just even a good old-fashioned romance?" I asked Missy on our drive. She laughed.

"To be honest, it's kind of a newer thing. I think Audrey, you know, the one who bit our heads off last time?" I remembered. "Audrey volunteers at the library but doesn't have many friends. Not hard to understand. But anyhow, she decided it would be good for women to have a safe place to meet and discuss books. Her husband left her a couple of years ago. They were so attached at the hip no one even saw it coming. Least of all Audrey. He just packed up and left. So her therapy was this book club and making the rest of us feel like shit if we break from protocol."

"Wow. You really are in the know."

"It's hard not to be. You have to choose to bury your head in the sand if you don't want to be. Our worlds all intermingle somehow. Either with kids. Or husbands. Or we went to school together. It's hard not to know the other's business."

"So no one ever leaves?"

"Most of us did. We went to colleges. Some went into the military. But it's a pretty amazing place to call home. I mean, I did get bored. But that was just an excuse. Even if most of our parents have passed away, it wouldn't feel right anywhere else."

"So, super personal question then. If everyone knows each other, how do you ever date or have hope for new love?"

"Sometimes, we cross the bridge and go to the other side." She looked at me and broke out into a big smile. Her lightheartedness made me laugh. "No, seriously. We go on dating apps. We do things outside of here, like work or sports. I suppose the bigger issue surfaces when we bring someone into our world on Sullivan's Island."

"So, people like me, don't just decide to move here."

"Nope. I mean, it can happen. Obviously, you did it. I think for most people, it's not on their radar. Like, how the hell did you end up here?"

I proceeded to tell her about my maiden name and Nicholas Sparks. She thought that was amusing and mostly spot on. "You can find love here."

"I know," I said. We had just pulled into the library parking lot. We grabbed our books and started to walk towards the entrance. She stopped in her tracks, processing.

"Wait. You know?" I smiled at her. "Who? You have to tell me."

I didn't want to tell her. Not yet, at least. I was happy she forgot that I had mentioned I met Beau. It was all so new. I thought about updating her on Beau, but we were about to walk into a room with Abby, and I didn't want her gloating in my favor. I couldn't tell her about Ben. I didn't know or, quite honestly, trust anyone enough with that information. I didn't even tell Emily about it. I could only imagine the cringe effect that would have had.

I was saved by Margo, who scurried from behind us with a modest-looking woman in tow. I did not recognize her from the last book club. "This is Dahlia. She's Janice's mom. The one who gave you the flier," Margo said. I shook Dahlia's hand.

"Nice to meet you. Janice had so many wonderful things to say about you," she said. Margo shot her a look, suggesting she had left out the part about my inaugural book club performance.

"She was so sweet, and my cottage is perfect," I said, doing my best to make a good impression.

"It should be. It has been in my family for a long time. Janice manages several of my properties. Most of them don't come up for lease often. Unless someone dies. Then, I suppose their misfortune is another's fortune. Like for you." She spoke so matter-of-fact I was having a hard time following. I didn't know what to say. "Don't worry, though. No one actually died in the house. So there aren't any evil spirits for you to ward off."

I looked at Missy for guidance. I couldn't read Margo. And I certainly didn't know what to think about Dahlia right now. "Thank you," I offered. All three of them started laughing.

"Oh, I'm sorry, Scarlet. You just made that way too easy." Her tone softened as if she might have taken the smallest liking to me. She wrapped her arm in mine as we walked towards the library entrance, Missy and Margo trailing behind. "Now, what brought you to our secret little town?"

"Divorce. New beginnings."

"Well, I hope it's to your liking so far."

"I love it." I did. I was happy here.

We walked into the same back room, and I looked around. The same women sat next to each other as last time, safeguarding their cliques so no one could break their bonds. I wondered who among them had contemplated a secret potion to eliminate their ex-husband.

I enjoyed reading "The Lost Apothecary" as it moved between two timelines. I was fascinated by the fact that it was chosen for book club. Were these women bitter enough to teeter on the verge of murder? Or did they simply like the premise that once upon a time, that might have been an option? Did they wish to live in the eighteenth century, when secret potions were blended to help women eliminate husbands and lovers?

Audrey gave our group an overly dramatic, clearly insincere hello as we walked in. She hugged Dahlia, Missy, and Margo. She made no effort to hug me. She looked me up and down and offered, "I'm so glad we didn't scare you off last time."

"I don't scare easily," I countered. She handed us each the list of questions for the book.

Dahlia went with Margo while Missy and I took the same seats from last time. "I hope we can stay out of the hot seat this week," Missy said, and we both began to giggle.

"Ladies," Audrey directed it towards us. "Let's settle down and get started."

"Let's get right to the meat and potatoes of this book. The first question tonight is: *What did you think about Nella's choice to start offering poison to women to kill the men who have wronged them?* Who'd like to start our discussion off?" I raised my hand. "Oh, Scarlet, honey, let someone else go first this week. Dahlia, what do you think?"

I looked at Missy. "Ouch," I said. She giggled. Audrey's eyes shot daggers. I put my finger over my smiling lips, "Shhhh."

Dahlia squirmed a little in her seat. It wasn't a tricky question. Even if she didn't read the book, she could give an opinion. She cleared her throat and then calmly began to answer. "I think the question could be a little incriminating. I mean, honestly, didn't most of us wish our husbands dead for being bastards and cheats?" The women began shaking their heads, some mumbling "amen" under their breaths. I squirmed. Shane wasn't a bastard or cheat. He might have wished me dead, killed unsuspectingly by a secret concoction of herbs. She continued, "Wasn't it Martha Coyles that got caught for this same thing?"

I looked at Missy for clarification. "Martha unsuccessfully tried to lace her husband's coffee with rat poison. It was kind of perfect, actually. He was an exterminator. But a major fucker. Like literally, fucking women all over the place." I raised my eyebrows. "On the other side. It's why it took so long for her to figure it out. But when she did, she was pissed."

Before I could ask what happened to Martha Coyles, Audrey chimed in. "Now, ladies, we are not supposed to gossip in our group. Martha was found not guilty of attempted murder. It was a shame, though, that Hugh was found dead in the bed of one of his lovers. I guess it served him right." Oh, this town of a couple thousand had ghosts in its closet.

Missy spoke. "If you ask me, it was perfect. No way Martha was letting him get away with what he did to her. Someone was going to pay along with Hugh."

"Missy, enough. Speculation is the devil's work."

I sometimes forgot I was in the South until references to God and church were made. And the morally rigid buried their heads in the sand. I applauded them for wanting to believe they were above the pettiness of gossip. It clearly lurked beneath the surface, and it took all their might to keep it repressed.

Dahlia spoke again. "I didn't mean to get us off subject. Even though that was very much on the subject. But I don't think most of us have it in us to want redemption. I say we are better off without liars, cheaters, or whatever our exes did."

Margo offered, "A man shouldn't mess with a woman scorned. But I think our words can be pretty toxic sometimes. Our exes know they were wrong—at least, the liars and cheats. But not everyone here is the victim of lying and cheating, so just wanting your husband dead for losing interest in you is a little harder to justify." Her eyes landed on Abby when she finished.

"I never wished Beau dead. I never wanted the divorce," she said, then added defensively, "It just didn't work anymore."

"For him," I heard Margo add.

Abby was steaming. "Yes, Margo. For him. I would still be married to him if people didn't plant seeds in his head that we weren't enough. We were enough."

Margo desperately wanted to respond, but Audrey cut her off. "I'm starting to rethink the whole divorce and marriage theme of our books. Maybe we need to read less personal novels." Audrey wasn't nearly as naïve as she came off.

Everyone felt a little on edge as we filed out. Abby led the charge out of the room. She could be seen storming down the street with steam coming from her horns. She walked in the opposite direction of Poe's. At that moment, I decided it would be the ideal night to experience Poe's since Abby would not be there.

Missy filled me in on the way there that most of the women in our book club had not been the ones to want out of their marriage. Some of their husbands cheated. Some lied. Some lied about cheating. Some just walked out, like Audrey's ex. Only Martha had attempted murder. And got away with it.

"And Margo? She slept with your husband."

"Margo has always been there to pick up the scraps we leave behind. Even in Kindergarten, she'd steal cookies we didn't finish. In high school, she dated the boys we would not date anymore. And then Cal went after her because of me. I know she was on top of the world for that. She always wanted him. He played her. He fucked her. And then he packed up and left. He didn't want any part of Sullivan's Island anymore. Won't even come here when the kids visit. He's probably embarrassed. I cheated on him first, and then he stooped to Margo's level."

"But you were best friends. And you're still friends. I'm not sure I could have been a loyal friend like that."

"Oh, I forgot that part. She's my cousin. And family is forgiven here." I raised an eyebrow at her. "Well, not really. But she did me a favor, to be honest. I feel kind of bad for her. I'm sure she would have loved to have an apothecary full of secret potions to take out Cal. I never wished evil upon him. He dug his own grave. I'm better off for it."

Margo did not come to Poe's this evening. Only Missy, Dahlia, and I made the trek. I was relieved. Dahlia sat with us, and as soon as we clinked glasses, she asked me my story. I cut to the chase.

"I was not the woman scorned. I scorned. I strayed. And I decided I liked the idea of starting over better than pretending to be happy in a marriage that felt empty. Didn't matter that he was good. Or that he didn't hurt me. I knew life was short, and I wasn't too old yet to think about starting over. So here I am."

Satisfied with that answer, "Well, I hope there's some serious sex that happens in my rental." Missy and I almost spit our drinks out.

"Well, that was direct," Missy said.

"We all wish the same thing, and you know it," Dahlia said.

I couldn't admit to Dahlia how much sex had already taken place in her two-bedroom beach cottage, but I acknowledged her. "I will do my best." I guzzled the rest of my drink and lifted my glass for another. Dahlia excused herself to the ladies' room.

Missy gave me a peculiar look. To which I replied, "She has no idea how much."

"Oh, I knew there was more. You radiate an I've been fucked good look."

"God, I hope not. That'd be kind of embarrassing."

"Okay. You radiate, which is much better than being bitter and angry and waiting for something to happen instead of making something happen."

"You radiate, too. You seeing someone?"

"Define seeing. I see a man naked a couple times a week. We have sex. We talk. We have more sex," she admitted.

"You are full of juicy goodness, aren't you? I knew I liked you as soon as you got me in trouble in class."

Dahlia sat back down. She held up her phone. "Janice needs me to help her with some stuff. I'll see you later, ladies." She fake-kissed us both goodbye.

"Dang, girl. Fake kiss from Dahlia on the day you met her. She must have sensed your just been fucked energy too."

We settled into a conversation about life, love, and kids. I felt I had found a person to call my friend here. I wasn't sure how much about Beau I should share. It was still a small town. We finished our drinks, paid, and began to walk out. I made a pit stop at the bathroom while Missy headed out front. When I came back out, I saw Missy talking with a man. He turned around as soon as Missy pointed. My draw dropped.

"Beau, I want you to meet Scarlet. She's new to town."

"I know Scarlet." He winked at me. I felt the tension ease, and I smiled at him. He leaned in and gave me a peck on the cheek.

"This is why I glow," I said.

"Okay, good. I like this," she said, drawing an imaginary circle around us. If she was caught off guard, she did not show it.

We small talked for a moment longer. Missy said she saw someone she knew inside and wanted to say hi. Beau and I went ahead without her. Seconds later, my phone pinged. "If Abby finds out, she'll have a shit...You go, girl." I replied with a heart emoji.

"All good?" Beau asked.

"So good." I grabbed his hand, and we began walking back to my place. "How'd you know I'd be there?"

"I was waiting on your steps to surprise you. I saw Abby storm by." He looked at me. "No, she did not see me. I figured if you weren't right behind, you probably went to Poe's. And if I was wrong, I'd likely bump into you on the way back."

"You sure you weren't a detective instead of fire chief?" He laughed. "I miss you when I'm not with you. That must be love, right?"

"Or a sex addiction. Because the sex..."

"You're right. It's the sex. Freaking mind-blowing sex."

"Thank God. I was worried you were falling in love with me. That's dangerous."

He stopped and pulled me in tight. "If falling in love with you is dangerous, I am all in."

SEVENTEEN

I LIKED SHARING my bed with Beau. I think there would be leftover space in a twin bed. Our bodies were always twisted in one another, constantly feeling the other person. There was genuine comfort in having him in my space, even if he snored on occasion, or I did, for that matter.

The newfound level of intimacy in my life brought about a desire to write poetry again. I hadn't done any serious writing of prose in a long time. I did it when I was younger and could express in writing what I couldn't articulate to my parents or friends. But now, I am finding a new appreciation for poetry. In the days and weeks Beau had come into my life, I had started playing with prose. He made me excited for words again. I found myself switching between painting and writing, wishing I had a musical bone in my body so that I could put the words to music.

Poetry, I told myself, didn't have to be complicated or have some deep-seated meaning. It could just be what I wanted. One afternoon, I found myself humming words

while I busied myself waiting for Beau. I had painted a
little that afternoon but kept losing focus. The painting
wasn't coming together like the words in my mind were.
I grabbed a pen and paper pad, and the words just flowed.

Stuck in a moment
Wishing for you
Stuck in that moment
Hoping it's true
Hearing you knocking
Drowning you out
Fearing tomorrow
Crashing in doubt
My head says hide
Don't let him inside
My heart says stay
Don't run away
A chance worth taking
A mistake worth making
The risk means opening up
Baring it all
Wanting to be more
Feeling so small
Can he love me for what I am?
Or will he see me as too far gone?
Will I scare him because I love too much?
Or will he want more because that's not enough?
My head says hide
Don't let him inside
My heart says stay

Don't run away
A chance worth taking
A mistake worth making

It was a start, and I felt satisfied that I had finished my first attempt. The words came quickly. I hadn't articulated those thoughts to anyone. I'm not sure I had even admitted them to myself. But I was lamenting my lack of musical talent. The poem had a melody in my head. If only I could write music or play an instrument, for that matter. Beau knocked on the door, jolting me from the pity party I had for myself that I lacked musical talent.

I felt like a schoolgirl every time I saw him. I threw my arms around him and kissed him hard on the lips. I didn't care that he had dinner in one hand and a bottle of wine in the other.

"Wow. That was a nice welcome."

"I missed you." He looked at his watch as if to remind me it hadn't been that long since he left. "I know. But I like it when you're here."

He walked in and put the bottle of wine in the refrigerator. He took out the cardboard to-go boxes on the counter. As he did, he noticed my notepad on the counter. He grabbed it and began to read. "What's this?" he asked when he finished it.

I wasn't embarrassed. I was actually kind of excited to learn what he thought. But then I panicked because what if he hated it? I didn't want to spin. I felt good about it. It made me feel good to write again.

"It's nothing really. Kind of silly. I haven't written poetry in a long time. But it felt really good." I watched him for a moment as he reread the words. The expression on his face went from contemplative to concerned.

"You hate it?" I asked.

"No. No. Just confused. I'm a mistake?"

I felt a wave of relief. "Who says this is about you?" He eyed me long after I said that.

"It's raw, whoever it's for."

"Thanks."

"It'd make a nice song." He could tell I was confused.

"I write music—a little. Or I used to, anyway. It's been a while." He took the poem and pointed to some of my words. "This could be the chorus." He hummed it, saying the words in a sing-song way. He was melting me more in that moment as the words of my poem were becoming real under his breath.

"Wow. You have a nice voice, Beau. Like really nice. And you made my words sound so beautiful."

"They are." He paused. "If it's any consolation, I get it. I understand them. What you're saying."

He put the pad down and turned to me. He stared at me, then brushed the strand of hair from my face, tucking it behind my ear. His thumb lingered on my cheek.

"Why do you scare me?" I finally asked.

"Because we're not little kids anymore. We have baggage. And it's sometimes more than we can carry." I laughed at how valid those words were.

"It's more than that," I said.

"I know. It's because I've fallen in love with you." He kissed me sweetly after he said the words.

"Is that why you scare me? You think I'm afraid to let you love me?" "No." He muffled his laugh under his breath. "You can't control that part. I already am loving you." *He was already loving me.* No one had ever said it to me like that before.

"I like that. I'm loving you too."

"Then, no more being scared."

"I cannot promise that." And I couldn't. I was more afraid that I might hurt him. If he learned about Ben. If Carter couldn't leave well enough alone. If Abby suddenly put all the pieces together. Would he still be loving me then?

He began kissing my neck and then found my lips, kissing them tenderly. He began pulling my blouse off my shoulders, exposing them, then gently ran his finger along my bra line, his lips lingering slowly behind. "I will just have to convince you otherwise."

"I would like that very much," I said quietly, under my breath, wanting to feel every part of his lips on me. "But we should eat first."

We sat at the counter, the words I had written on the paper pad before us. Our knees touched, our hands brushed each other, and kisses shared between sips of wine. He was thinking.

"I really like what you wrote."

"First stab. Did you ever write poetry?" I asked.

"Of course. As a teenager. You know, that teenage angsty kind of stuff," he replied. "The weight of the world on our weak shoulders. There was some deep shit at times."

"Of course. Life was terminal then."

"It still is," he said with a smile.

"Touche. But you know. We were all dying in our teenage years. Really. Did you ever think back then that you'd live to be this old?"

He smiled and chuckled at that. "I wanted to live forever," he said. "I still do."

"So you were basically the anti-teenager?"

"Not exactly. I had hard times, too. I guess I just never let shit bother me to the degree other kids did. I recognized early on that life was short."

"Pretty perceptive for a kid. Good for you."

He thought about it longer.

"I had a brother, though," he paused, seemingly crafting the word order in his mind. "He was all the angst. All the drama. All the emotions. Until he wasn't. And I told myself I would never be that person. I would find good and happy even in all the shit."

"He killed himself?" I asked. He didn't leave me a choice. I didn't want to assume. I had hoped I was wrong.

"And I found him. Hanging in the garage. When I opened it. I was twelve. He was fifteen. And it sucked. My parents never got over it."

"I don't imagine you would."

"No. But it was his choice. They weren't bad parents. I wasn't a bad brother. His world wasn't bad. But it was to him. So he chose to end it." I watched as he told me the story. I could feel both his anger and sadness.

"My parents couldn't handle it and got divorced within a year. They both blamed each other. I'm surprised they never blamed me. But they didn't. At least they didn't fuck that up. It's actually how I ended up here. My mom left and took me with her. We moved into my grandparents' house. They died a few years later. It was just the two of us in this big old house on the water. Then she died. Then, when Abby and I divorced, the house was all I wanted. It was the good from the fucked up part of losing my brother. I think it was pretty cathartic for me and my mom. My dad had a harder time. And we didn't have much contact until the very end. I think he blamed himself for everything. And, really, no one was to blame. I tried to make sure I took that lesson with me into parenting my own kids. And then especially with the divorce."

He had just shared an enormous amount of deeply personal information with me that I was trying to digest. My adoration of this man became greater at that moment as I learned of the emotional hurdles he had overcome to get here, doing so with a smile on his face and gratitude in his heart.

"That's a lot. Thanks for sharing that."

"Not many people know that part of the story."

"I don't imagine it's something you run around telling people. It's a heavy burden for a young boy to carry."

"My mom couldn't talk about it. She was so stoic. But she loved me. Maybe too much," he said, laughing.

"Well, in my very not important opinion, you turned out awesome. And your kids turned out great, right?"

"They are works in progress." He snickered.

"Mine too," I added. "But I was never that full of angst that I considered..." How were you supposed to word that without making it seem trivial? "...that I considered non-existence an option."

"Like with so many things in life, resentment requires a lot of energy I don't want to expend. On my brother, my parents, and even Abby." Under his breath, I heard him say, "That one is still a work in progress."

I BELIEVED Beau was in love with me and that what we had was more profound than good sex. It became clear to me that intimacy on both an emotional and physical level was what we had quickly evolved to. I couldn't remember having that with Shane, maybe ever, but certainly not the last several years of our marriage when I needed it most.

But there were moments when I felt deep-seated self-doubt begin to climb from where I had hoped it would never be unearthed. He gave me no reason to question, but insecurity is an awful thing. Finding a way to accept my current reality could be a struggle some days. I hoped my moments of feeling I wasn't enough for this wonderful man didn't make him frustrated with my sometimes-backward progress.

I embraced Beau sharing about life with Abby. We both needed to know our stories to nurture our own. It was who we were and how we had gotten to this point. Like most of us, I knew he and Abby weren't perfect. But it was clear that he once had a profound love for her. They shared interests. They laughed. "We were right together until we weren't. I think she might have had a mental breakdown. Started making shit up. Maybe her friends were feeding her stuff, and she believed them. Maybe that asshole Donovan thought he could have her."

"Wait. Who's Donovan?"

"Donovan was a family friend. We had a group of friends whose kids were all the same age. We did a lot of things together. Don's wife passed away when the kids were teenagers. Abby stepped up to help out. I think he fell for her. And I think she liked the attention."

"Abby does not give the impression she had an affair."

"Of course not. She never admitted it to me, either. But I found stuff that would make me think otherwise."

"That sucks."

"Yup. But he moved a few years ago after his kids went to college. I had money on her going with him. It would have made my life a hell of a lot easier. And cheaper." He looked at me and laughed. "I really hoped she'd marry that son of a bitch. But, at the end of the day,

I loved Abby. She was good to me. She talked to me. She was a great mom. She got lost. We got lost. The ending is a blur."

I embraced him sharing his story, but I would hiccup, wondering how I was ever going to match, let alone exceed, some expectation predicated on his first wife, the one I knew he truly loved once, the one whose shadow covered me in fear that I would never be enough.

I was honest with Beau about my occasionally volatile and precarious insecurities about myself. I didn't want him to think it was him. I had always struggled with not feeling like I was good enough. I could hide those feelings in the years the kids were being raised. But divorce reminded me of my weaknesses and made me question whether I was worthy or deserving of more. I shared these things with Beau. He never laughed at me or told me what I felt was stupid, didn't discount them as trivial.

"I get it," he told me one night after I admitted my insecurities and internal fears of trying to be better than Abby. "You don't have to be better than anyone. The situations are so different. You are the best for me now, at this point. I am so happy with you. I didn't think I could be this happy again. We both bring shit to the party. Heck, our shit has shit. It would be unrealistic to think either one of us is perfect."

Beau. Of all the men I never saw myself meeting or falling in love with. He was worth trying to let go of my self-perceived inadequacies.

"You're pretty perfect," I said.

"Really? I'm not some old geezer to you?"

"Hah. I finally found your insecurity." He rolled his eyes. "Age is just a number. I don't feel like we're ten years apart. You don't look or act like an old man." I smiled coyly at him.

"So, perfect, huh?"

"Well, I mean, perfect would be six feet tall so that I could wear high heels, and you'd weigh at least thirty pounds more than I do, so I wouldn't freak out that someday I may weigh more than you. But, yes, pretty damn perfect."

"Ditto...Well, except for the whole thing about my height and weight. I've always just been average in that department." We laughed. As we always do, which is why it felt perfect with him. I kissed him on the cheek.

"You are so not average."

EIGHTEEN

IN EVERY RELATIONSHIP, there is a coming out. It's the time when you no longer hide from the world. You stop finding secret places to eat. You no longer look over your shoulder to see who might be watching. Sullivan's Island was small. Beau was well known. Hiding was not something we would be able to do forever. And, if I had to be honest with myself, there was some relief in knowing he would want to be seen in public with me. It was like a proclamation that he wasn't ashamed of me or afraid of potential gossip. Not that I had any reason to believe that's what he thought. I just tripped over my own thoughts sometimes.

While Beau and I had been out many times together, it wasn't in the usual places. We enjoyed each other's company in the quiet of the less visited locales. He was less likely to run into people he knew. But even I was starting to see familiar faces. Daily errands to the same places: grocery store, hardware store, coffee shop. A town this small breeds familiarity. I would occasionally see one of the women from book club who might wave or even offer a quick *hello, how are you?* To me, that felt like progress. I had Missy, the friend I couldn't have imagined who shared a similar past and embraced the liberation of being divorced and free to choose her own path.

We weren't wearing T-shirts that said *he's mine, and I'm his.* We weren't flaunting being a couple. We were open and affectionate. He held my hand whenever we went out. He'd occasionally lean in, kiss me sweetly, or rest his hand on my leg. I liked the subtle public displays of affection. He would introduce me to people he knew if the situation warranted. It felt official and like the most natural thing in the world.

Along with our coming out as Beau and Scarlet, I wondered what we were supposed to call us as a couple. We weren't young, which fit the label of boyfriend and girlfriend. Do we introduce each other as partners? That worked, but when the other wasn't there, and I said *my partner and I,* did I have to immediately qualify it with the proper pronoun or clarify it wasn't a business relationship? Too much potential for clarification there. We could be significant others. Even that implied a deeper level of commitment. We were old. There should be a label for older people dating and falling in love.

We were lying in bed, me resting my head on his chest. I liked it there. Beau didn't have a hairy chest, just enough that I could lightly run my fingers through it and run my pointer finger around his nipples. Earlier that evening, we had dinner front and center at High Thyme. It was the first time going back since we had dinner with Emily. And Carter unexpectedly showed up. This time, it was just the two of us sitting at a table for two, affectionate with one another. Holding hands. Laughing. Smiling. I never stopped smiling when I was with him.

"I love how your eyes light up. They're so expressive," he said.

"Thank you. I can say the same about yours." He smiled. "I like us. I like this."

"What is this? Like what are we?"

"What do you mean?"

"Like, what's the label?"

"Do we need one?" He asked. I wasn't sure we did. But there was an awkwardness to talking about someone you're with and not being able to clearly identify what that relationship is. "You wanna go steady?" He jokingly asked.

"Ewww. So seventies and eighties."

"Will you be my girlfriend?"

"Also, so weird. Right? It's like we're not young anymore. There needs to be a word for older people."

"Significant other. Partner. Non-spouse. Person."

"See my point?" I asked.

"I do now. I don't think I've given it much thought before. Maybe there's a German word for it somewhere. They have uber-descriptive words for everything."

"Obviously. I haven't had a reason to think about it before, either." It was true. I didn't pay much attention to what my divorced acquaintances called their partners. It just sounded strange when I thought about what my relationship with Beau was becoming.

"I know. It just came to me. Will you be *my* Scarlet?"
It was simultaneously corny and sweet.

"Only if you'll be *my* Beau."

I liked that for us. It felt uniquely ours.

There were so many parts to being with Beau, of loving him, that felt different. The part I didn't expect about finding love later in life was the part where you didn't have to hurry. We could lie naked in bed for hours, touching each other, loving each other, laughing, talking about lifetimes lived and lessons learned. When in my life had I ever had hours in a day to do nothing? To be genuinely lost in those moments as they were happening, oblivious to the clock ticking or the outside world waiting.

There would be beauty to finding love later, for being afforded second chances when we thought there were none for the taking. Our bodies were fluid, flowing freely from one moment to the next. Laughter became making love, which became conversation, and then making love again. We flowed. It was easy. Seamless. The perfect connection of our bodies and minds transitioning so smoothly in those moments that it wasn't clear when one began and the other ended.

WE SAT on the back deck, drinking our coffee in agreeable silence. The mornings overlooking the quiet of the ocean were like meditation. It filtered my mind, cleared the cobwebs, and allowed me to start my day with a clean slate. I liked that I rarely needed a long checklist of things to do in a day. Sometimes, I wondered if I kept long lists before as a form of distraction; the need to always be going and accomplishing things was just a way to avoid facing the reality of my life. I liked this new slower pace. And starting mornings with Beau was an unexpected bonus.

"The annual Sullivan's Island Lighthouse Preservation Society fundraiser, Jesus, that's a mouthful, is Saturday. You'll be there, right?" He said so matter of fact.

"Missy mentioned it. She asked me to be her plus one. I said I would. And you didn't ask."

"I do not enjoy fundraisers. I ignore them as long as possible. I'm on the board, though, so I gotta be there. Please don't read anything into me going solo." He kissed me on the neck. "Missy will be much better company."

"Yes, we will sit on our perch and observe Sullivan's Island society schmooze," I said with a small pit in my stomach, knowing that women from my book club would be there. Who was I kidding? They would all be there. Beau and I had already come out as a couple. At least we weren't hiding it. It was a small town. We knew people would gossip. If we owned up to it, it would be one less thing for anyone to wonder about. But did he suddenly have reservations in a spotlight situation when eyes would be on us?

"I will be keeping an eye on you, my Scarlet."

"And I, you, my Beau." I liked the sound of that.

"And I will likely find it difficult to keep my hands off of you, so expect me to seek you out at various times throughout the evening."

"You don't worry about being seen with me?" He rolled his eyes at me. "No, seriously. I know we aren't hiding this from anyone. But this is a lot of people you know in one place. I would understand if you wanted to downplay it a little."

"While I appreciate that, I am excited to share our relationship. I just don't want you stuck waiting for me when I have obligations. You'll have a much better time with Missy."

He grabbed my empty coffee cup and got up. He planted a kiss on my head before going in. "Assuming you'd like another?"

"You know me so well." Beau left and returned a few moments later with two fresh cups of Nespresso. Coffee was one of life's great joys. I took the cup as he handed it to me. "Thank you."

"Of course." He paused. "So I just saw the pad of paper on the counter."

"I'm guilty of lots of pads. I like lists."

"It looked like you've been writing again."

The poem I had started yesterday before seeing Beau. The poem about my heart racing and gasping for air. I looked at him.

"I wasn't snooping. I swear. It was there." He was defending himself for no reason.

"I started it before you got here. I was..." I stopped suddenly, embarrassed by what I wanted to say next.

"Go on. You can't leave me hanging. The little bit I couldn't help but read was lovely."

"I was trying to think of how to make it be a song. A love song. About us."

"I like that you're finding inspiration to write these really cool poems."

"You're kind of inspiring," I said.

"I just wish you weren't questioning so much. See me as the answer to your happily. No doubts."

"I have a lifetime of questioning my place. I am a work in progress. The last year has taught me that it doesn't matter how much you anticipate, plan, or think you've figured it out. There's a curve ball here, a bump there, a brick wall. Life doesn't come with warning labels. We...I tend to create them over time. We...I heed the ones we...I choose to while ignoring the ones screaming at us...me the loudest. I can be my own worst enemy. And I'm trying to be kinder to myself. But every so often, insecure me takes hopeful me down a negative path."

"How nice for you, though, to have outlets. You have your art. You have poetry. And whatever else you're writing."

"Have you been snooping in my office?" I said jokingly.

"No, I have not. I remember you saying you would be doing all sorts of writing." He was right. The freelance writing I did was mundane and lacked much creativity. Two articles I submitted to The Huffington Post months ago were recently picked up. It motivated me and gave my confidence a little boost. While I hadn't started writing anything yet, I had started putting ideas to paper. And that was satisfying, too.

"I have lots of paper pads in there, too," I said in fun. "Lots of ideas. They get me excited. I just struggle to focus some days. I met this guy," I nuzzled up to Beau. "And he makes it really hard to concentrate sometimes."

"I can be around less."

"Hah. No chance. You're also my inspiration."

He finished off his coffee and got up from his chair. "As long as I don't end up in any books."

"Not making any promises."

Beau had a busy day of fundraiser preparation. We said our goodbyes, and I readied for my swim. I loved being this close to the ocean. I loved knowing I could walk out and lose myself whether I was in it or near it. I could feel it call to me. I had debated forgoing today's swim but knew that a swim would relax me and help me forget that I was scared to death inside for tonight's event.

I looked forward to seeing Beau in a suit and tie. I imagined he would look the part of a distinguished board member. Before moving, I considered donating the few cocktail dresses and limited formal wear from my years at the Oceanside Museum of Art. I was glad I did not.

NINETEEN

MISSY WAS HER EVER-PUNCTUAL SELF. I told her I could go to the fundraiser myself, but she insisted on making a grand entrance together.

She did not knock or ring the doorbell. I heard the front door open and a loud proclamation, "Your chariot awaits, madam." I could hear her giggle. "Scarlet? Scar? Where are you?"

"I'm in my room."

She came through the door, and my mouth dropped. She was wearing an emerald green floor-length gown with a slit halfway up her thigh. Off the shoulders. Tight fitting. Four-inch heels. And her red hair perfectly falling off her shoulders.

"Holy smokes. You look hot."

"Right?"

"Hello, modesty?"

"Overrated. When you know you've got it, you gotta work it."

I was struggling with which outfit to wear. I had three dresses on my bed. I had tried them all on at least three times, taken selfies, and sent them to Emily for consult. Yet, I stood there in my bra and panties when Missy walked in.

"So, this wouldn't work, would it?" I asked, waving my hands like Vanna White up and down my body.

"In a strip club." I laughed.

"But your hair and make-up look spot on." It was a consolation prize. I was never a big make-up girl, but I could put together my look when needed. The more challenging part was finding make-up that didn't dive into my nooks and crannies.

She looked at each of the dresses. The black one was too expected. The blue one was too understated. She held up the burgundy one. It was one of my favorites. It was simple and timeless: a strapless midi dress that tied at the back and had a slit up the side. I put it on, and Missy just smiled.

I had a pair of lower wedge heels that completed my outfit. It was a new issue I found myself contending with. I was barely shorter than Beau. It wasn't that I was overly tall at my scarcely five foot seven height, which I will confess has likely come down to five foot six. I've learned we really do shrink as we age. I never worried about that with Shane. And I don't think Beau cared if I was inches taller than he was. Some men even found a taller woman sexy. I was not that woman who would be okay with that, even if he was. I did not need extra attention drawn to me in the name of being taller than the man. Fortunately, my heels looked perfect with the dress. And my feet would not be cursing me minutes into the evening.

"Nailed it!" Missy exclaimed as I stood in front of the mirror for a final look. "Now, get your purse and make haste. Tonight is going to be so much fun."

"It's a fundraiser. How fun can that be?"

"It's *the* fundraiser. Everyone will be there. It's our who's who of Sullivan's Island."

"Population 2000." I was being snarky.

"Just you wait. It'll be a blast. And it's kind of like a cotillion for you."

Like I wasn't already nervous about seeing the women from book club. Mostly Abby. How would she react to seeing me and Beau together? I had an uneasy feeling in my gut that went beyond the realization that I had forgotten to eat most of the day.

WE ARRIVED A HALF HOUR LATE, which was fashionably on time. We pulled up to a beautiful, old mansion on the oceanfront. "Do people still live here?" I asked.

Missy explained that it belonged to one of the founding families of Sullivan's Island. "This is their summer home, it's rumored. Not sure where they live the rest of the time. They have some freaky family stuff." She shrugged her shoulders. "Once a year, they open their doors, and we see how the other side lives."

We left her car at the valet, then walked the stone staircase lined with brightly colored rose bushes to the front of the house, where two sharp-looking gentlemen in tuxedos opened the doors for us. Inside, we were met with champagne flutes. The home spared no expense or detail. Two staircases ascended from either side of the foyer. The centerpiece of the entrance was a spectacular antique chandelier hanging to the center of the room. Marble floors led to a giant ballroom. Maybe it was ordinarily a living room - or three. It was glamorous and filled with beautifully dressed women and sharply clad men. I looked to see if I could glimpse Beau, but he was nowhere to be seen.

Missy introduced me to people she knew as we headed towards the beachside of the mansion. I needed food, and it was in good supply. Missy went to get us drinks as I perused through the various food tables. I filled my tiny plate, avoiding looking around. I could feel myself being watched. I was paranoid; I knew that. I had done nothing wrong other than offend a few thin-skinned women in book club. I was not having an affair with a married man; I was dating an eligible bachelor.

I waited at a table for Missy to return, inhaling my food. An empty stomach and alcohol would not bode well for me. It was a preemptive strike on my part. As I did, I finally dared to look around, see the faces, and take in my first South Carolina fundraiser. I smiled at Missy across the room as she held up two wine glasses. I mouthed, "Thank God." As I did, I felt an arm come around me from behind, immediately followed by lips on my neck. Beau. I smiled, a sense of ease overcoming me.

"Wow. You look stunning," he said, grinning like a teenage boy at his first homecoming dance.

"Thank you. You clean up nicely," I teased back. Missy walked up, handed me my drink, and shared an air cheek kiss with Beau.

"You look lovely, Missy."

"Dapper as always, Mr. Sanders." He chuckled.

"This is an incredible setup," I said.

"The haunted house of Sullivan's Island never disappoints when hosting an event," Beau said. "I hope you have a lovely time, ladies, but I must go do business." He nodded to a group of stodgy old men standing not far from us. He kissed me sweetly and left. He changed gears quickly. I admired that.

Missy and I spent the next hour walking the room. She introduced me to the people she knew, which seemed to be almost everyone. She worked the room, confident and playful, and knew something about everyone. People were excited to see her and lit up as she approached. They were happy to meet me, and I didn't feel judged. Being with her made me relax. Knowing Beau always had an eye towards my direction was reassuring as well.

Missy and I stood at the bar, momentarily in place while we sipped our wine. I was glad I had eaten earlier. "You literally know everyone," I said.

"I've lived here forever."

"So has half this town, and I don't think most of them are represented. Everyone you've introduced me to is some sort of who's who and not just from here."

She took a big sip. "My parents – and ex – were kind of big shots." I looked at her. "Yes, I come from a wealthy family, to answer your question. I inherited most of it. And because Cal wasn't necessarily well-liked, I think people might have felt sorry for me. Except," she laughed. "Except for the women in our book club. I suppose I kind of wanted to be part of that as an in-your-face for thinking I didn't deserve to continue to hold my place in our tiny little society."

"This is exactly how I stereotyped the south. Not going to lie," I admitted.

"When I cheated on Cal, I knew that shit could hit the fan. And it did. But I was intent not to let life dictate the outcomes. We all make concessions. So many people get lost in the process. I did not want to be that woman." She looked at me. "Can I tell you something?"

"Of course." Always hated that question. It's a loaded, potentially double-edged sword.

"I was so grateful when you showed up, and we became friends. I felt this weight lifted as if I didn't have to carry this burden alone anymore. You got it. You understood."

I was choked up. I wiped my eyes in hopes I did not leak a tear. "I lived that."

"Okay, enough sappy confessions. Did you notice Audrey, Margo, and Abby in the corner? They're watching us like hawks. They have barely moved since getting here."

Just as I was about to ask her if she thought Abby had seen me with Beau, he came up next to me, wrapping his arm around my waste. "Dance with me, Scar." It was not a question. I handed Missy my drink, and he held my hand as we made our way to the center of the large banquet room. It reminded me of European castles (and the Haunted House at Disneyland). I imagined there had once been a fifty-foot table in the center of the room, flanked by a hundred velvet-covered chairs. There was a small chamber orchestra of fifteen musicians in the corner. They played a fun mix of modern classical music reminiscent of "Bridgerton" balls. We danced to Miley Cirus's "Wrecking Ball." *Could there be a more fitting piece?* I wondered. Beau and I laughed and smiled as we awkwardly attempted to synchronize our feet.

"Oh, Beau, this is awful. I'm sorry," I said.

"Are you kidding? This is the most fun I have ever had dancing at one of these things." He pulled me in tight, stopped dancing momentarily, and kissed me on the dance floor. It was the most cliché, kitschy high school dance moment ever. "God, I love you," he said. I was beaming.

"I love you, back."

"Thank God," he said jokingly. "And now I have to get back, but I just wanted a few stolen moments with you." He kissed my cheek, winked at me, and walked off. As he did, I was met with Abby's evil glare. Missy swooped in, grabbed me by the arm, and gave an "in your face" look to Abby. It was hard not to find Missy endearing.

"Seriously, that man has fallen hard for you," she said quietly.

"It goes both ways."

"And the look on Abby's face was worth the price of admission alone. I need to pee." And off she went, leaving me standing in a sea of people. No one but me seemed to care, so I headed to the food table. It felt safe, slightly out of the line of fire. I stuffed a mini quiche and two slices of Gouda into my mouth. It was heaven. I filled a glass with cucumber mint water and chased down my food. I refilled the glass, feeling the need to refrain from more alcohol. When I turned around, my eyes locked on Ben, who was looking at me. He smiled and then pointed towards the outside. How did I miss that he was here? He had to be the youngest in the room, save for the awkward teenagers whose parents made them come. I never saw him with Beau. Or Abby, for that matter.

Missy had stopped before reaching me and was enjoying the attention of several of the much older, age-inappropriate board members. She did not see me walk off behind Ben. I looked to see if anyone else did either. I was being paranoid. No one knew about me and Ben. There would be no reason for anyone to suspect us. Beau had his back turned and was laughing with a group. I didn't see Abby or any of the other book club women.

I followed as he walked through a large slider that opened to a stunning English garden on the side of the house. The owners spared no expense in creating a magical haven. I wondered why it had a haunted stigma associated with it. The fact that it was big, old, and unoccupied most of the time made me think it was just a stereotype associated with these kinds of homes.

Once outside, Ben stopped and turned towards me. He leaned in, gently kissing my cheek. "You look beautiful, Scarlet. Like, really beautiful."

"Ben, I..." He interrupted me.

"Nope. I didn't come here for anything. I just wanted to let you know I have an amazing opportunity in Florida. I wanted to say goodbye in person before I left."

"That's so exciting for you." I felt a rush of relief at the thought that crossing paths with Ben in the future would not be a regular occurrence that I would dread only because of the potential truths that might be exposed.

"And I wanted to tell you how much I loved being with you. You really are an amazing woman."

"You're making me blush," I said in fun. "You will make a woman so lucky someday. You made me feel like a younger version of myself. Like I wasn't old."

He muffled a laugh. "I never ever once thought you were old."

"I know. But I did. It was fun. And liberating. I needed you. You helped me find me. And then, of course,..."

"My dad."

"I'm crazy for him."

"I know. And he's crazy for you."

"He can never know."

"I know. I'll never make it weird. I'd never do that to my dad. He deserves to be happy." He looked at me with his gorgeous face and those eyes that were unquestionably his father's. "I hope I find someone like you."

"Younger." I couldn't resist.

"A little," he said, winking at me. "I like the parts where you know yourself."

"That was a journey, and time gave me the tools to figure that out," I said.

He leaned in and whispered in my ear, "I'll never call you mom, though."

I pulled back, giggling, "God, I hope not."

Ben kissed me sweetly on the cheek. Our fingers brushed softly as he pulled away. I watched as he walked out of sight. I turned to go back inside and was met by Abby's evil glare. Our eyes met for a moment before she turned away. I swear I could see the fumes coming from her head. I had no choice but to follow her back inside.

Abby marched over to Beau. She did not make a scene. She was animated while speaking, her hands flailing in front of Beau's face. His expression did not change, but he was listening. I watched in horror from across the room. Our eyes met. He put his drink down, grabbed his coat from the table, and began walking towards the door. Without me.

I felt my world crashing down at that moment. The man I loved had just discovered I might have had something with his son. He didn't know the story, the timing, or if it was true. Whatever Abby told him was based on speculation of a moment she witnessed between me and Ben.

I hurried after Beau. "Beau, can we talk about it?" I called out to him once we were outside. He waved me off as he left. I felt Missy put her arm through mine as she turned me back to the party. "He'll be fine," she offered.

"I'm not so sure," I said as I saw the look of satisfaction on Abby's face when we returned. At least Abby had the dignity not to shout it out to the entire fundraiser.

The following two hours were a painful exercise in pretending to be something I was not. I was not happy. I did not want to be there. I wanted to curl up and hide in a hole.

TWENTY

I TRIED my best to hide. I hoped Beau would be there waiting for me when I returned from the fundraiser. He was not.

I woke the following morning hoping he'd bring me coffee in bed. He did not.

The next several days were agony. I texted Beau. No response. I called. It went straight to voicemail. I busied myself in a constant state of nausea. My morning swims did not bring me my usual perspective and clarity. Instead, they were clouded with a million "if only" s. If only I hadn't gone to the fundraiser. If only I didn't sleep with Ben. If only I didn't move here. If only. If only. If only. I was beating myself up.

My mind was spinning beyond just Beau and me. I imagined Abby had quickly enlightened the entire town about how horrible I was. I reminded myself I wasn't that important; why would anyone really care? I knew I had done nothing wrong. Ben and I were adults. Had I embarrassed Beau with the revelation? Is that why he was silent?

I avoided making trips into town, opting to drive over the bridge and run errands as far away as possible. Mostly, I stayed at home, bunkered in my studio, attempting to make art. But with every brush on the canvas, I felt myself choosing dark, gloomy colors. They were sad and depressing. I did not want to create art of despair. I wanted my art to be inspirational, hopeful, and happy.

I attempted writing. That, too, went down dark roads. I was in a new chapter of my life. I was getting to be me, a new version. 3.0. I didn't want my writing to depict anything other than that. I decided it was not a good time to write. Instead, I dove into books. Maybe I could lose myself in other people's words instead of my own. Book club was on Thursday. There was no way in my mind that I would be going. I picked up "Verity" from my stack of books and plowed through it anyway. The book clubbers will have a blast with that one, I thought.

I texted Missy that I would not be joining her this week. That did not go over well.

"You cannot leave me with the wolves," she texted back.

"You could choose not to go, too," I reminded her.

"Where's the fun in that? They'll be talking about you, and I want to hear what they say."

Dot, dot, dot.

She quickly followed that up with "LOL and JK."

"Not funny," I replied.

"Fine. But you know it's better if we go. Rip the band-aid off."

"I've been hemorrhaging just thinking about it," I said.

"I'll pick you up tomorrow."

Dot, dot, dot.

"End of discussion," she texted and added a kiss emoji.

"Waving the white flag." I wanted to add a middle finger emoji, but I knew she was right. I would have to face Abby and her posse eventually. I knew there would never be a right time. I promised myself I would be quiet, non-confrontational, a good girl. I could do that.

***

I WAS nervous about going to book club tonight. After the fundraiser, experiencing that moment with Abby, I feared the worst. "I've got your back," Missy promised. My look said *ugh*. Missy and I each had a glass of wine to ease the pain before we left.

I did not tell Missy the details of why Abby shot me a look or why Beau was so angry. She assumed it was because Abby saw Beau and me together. I don't imagine that was a friendly look then, either. I also didn't tell her I hadn't heard from Beau since that night. It had been five days. I drove by his house—empty, his car gone. I wanted proof of life and got none. My stomach was in knots.

"Fine, but I'm not saying anything," I said stubbornly.

"Of course. You don't have to participate. Just be there. It's like taking a stand. You will not be intimidated."

"She didn't bully me. She just scared the shit out of me. In the morning, I put a drop of my coffee on a paper towel to ensure it doesn't burn a hole in it just in case she secretly snuck in and poisoned it."

"Seriously? You need to get over yourself, girlfriend." She was probably right. In fact, I knew she was. Beau had told me the same thing. But neither of them was new to town, trying to make friends; but, instead, making enemies and bad impressions. "Besides, it's "Verity." Kind of dark. Twisted. Romance."

"Killing your kid? Pretending to be a vegetable?" We looked at each other and simultaneously said, "Or not."

"See? This is going to be so much fun," she said.

I crossed my arms over my chest like a defiant child, pouting as I said, "Fine."

We walked into the same room at the library, and it was like Groundhog Day all over. These people really did like their routines. I couldn't understand how these women could read so much. I wasn't sure I could keep up with the frenetic tempo they held. Granted, they weren't reading books on Einstein's Theory of Relativity or trying to understand Quantum Physics. But I wasn't sure I could keep the whole read-a-book twice-a-month thing going.

As we walked into the room, it fell silent. Absolute, complete silence. The women turned towards us, scowls frozen on their faces. Their looks were directed at me. Daggers unleashed. I could feel every single one as it entered my body. It was agony. Missy looked at me. Looked at them.

"What the hell is wrong with you people?" Missy yelled. I wondered if she could see the blood seeping through my clothes.

Audrey spoke first. "Missy, you really need to pick better friends."

"This is fucking book club," Missy snapped at her.

"Language, please. There are children at the library." She looked around at the usual cast of characters. Abby stood front and center, doing a terrible job trying to conceal her smug satisfaction at the assault on me.

"You're right, Audrey. You are children. Scarlet has every right to be here."

"It's just that some members have expressed discomfort with her presence."

"Seriously. Who?" I was mute. I'd never had a friend stand up for me before. Honestly, I never thought I would need one at this age.

Abby stepped forward. "It is an unwritten understanding of book club that we will not steal other women's men."

Missy's mouth fell. "So, Margo sleeps with my husband and..."

Margo's jaw dropped. "And, let's see, do I start calling out some others?" They were quiet. "This is a witch hunt. Shouldn't we just be happy that one of us is having sex?"

"Melissa!" Audrey admonished.

"Seriously. If it weren't for Abby and her unwillingness to accept Beau didn't want to be with her anymore, we'd all be happy for Scarlet. But Abby has some evil grip on all of you. If Beau chooses to be with someone else, and who can blame him, then Abby just needs to accept it."

The room was quiet. "Oh, no one has anything to say? Great. Then let's talk about this fucking book."

"Melissa. Again. Language."

She took a couple of deep breaths and went to sit down. I stood there. Frozen. Unable to comprehend what was happening. Abby looked right at me. "This isn't about Beau. And she knows it. And so do the rest of us." Missy looked at me. They all did. It took all I had to turn myself around and walk out.

I heard Missy calling after me, moving faster than she was used to, juggling her bag and "Verity" still firmly in her hand. I kept moving after she caught up to me. Once we were far removed from the library, we stopped. "Oh, thank God. I really need to start working out more."

We sat down on the bench by the park. Kids were still running around. Young moms were sitting on blankets chatting while their little ones toddled around. Once Missy had caught her breath, she said," Okay, that was awful. What the hell just happened in there?"

I was on the verge of tears. I took a deep breath and exhaled loudly. "I met someone when I first got here. Someone much younger. And God, it was fun. I got caught up in that moment. I think you can guess who."

She was silent for a moment, mouth agape. I took my finger and gently closed her mouth. "Oh, shit. It was Ben?" I didn't reply. She knew the answer. "Ben. Huh."

"Abby saw him talking to me at the fundraiser. I was telling him how much I loved Beau. And he was happy for me. But Abby must have seen him lean in to give me a kiss that meant nothing. I'm sure she could read the situation. We had a lot of chemistry. You know me cradle robbing and all."

"Jesus, Scar. I'm actually surprised you are still alive. If ever there were grounds to kill. I mean her husband and her son."

"Ex. Husband. And I didn't know any of that when it started. I mean, honestly, there was this part of me that worried if someone saw me and Ben or me and Beau that they'd secretly start plotting against me. There is no rule book on this whole post-divorce dating thing. I was trying to be in the moment and not worry about what others thought. But my worst fear just came true. I was publicly shamed and flogged in the unassuming library of Sullivan's Island."

"Really. You are a bit dramatic." If looks could kill, she might have been gutted in that moment. "Actually, that's some pretty heavy drama. I'm still trying to wrap my head around Ben. I get Beau." I looked at her. "Hello? He's old man hot. But Ben. He's just *hot*." She was right.

"I swear, even before tonight, I felt like every time I walked into book club, I had some letter emblazoned on my chest, like some big scarlet letter that says I am the anti-woman scorned. The scorner. The bad guy. The evil witch. So many names I could call myself."

Missy gave me a quizzical look. "No, really. I feel like an alphabet is rotating across my chest in that room with those women."

"I wanna hear it. Go." I was ready.

"A for adulterer, B for bitch, C for cunt, D for divorcee."

"We're all that. Keep going," she interjected.

"E for evil. F for fucked. G for God, she's annoying. H for harlot. I for infidel or idiot." I shot her a look. "Can I stop now? I do enough self-reflection as it is."

"Yea. After all that, I need a drink. And maybe a shower."

"Let's go to my house and open a bottle of wine, please. I don't want to be in public right now. I just want space from humans."

"If it helps, I don't think any worse of you. I actually really appreciate and like your candor. And now that I know you rolled in the hay with Ben, I pretty much revere you." That made me laugh out loud. She was trying to lighten my mood, but Abby's accusations had eaten away at me.

"Do you think we become untrustworthy because we cheated?" I asked in earnest. "Do we ever lose the cloak of potential infidelity?"

"No. I don't think so. We're awesome people. We just need to remind ourselves of that. I mean, that's not to say some people will always get distracted. But I don't think they're the norm. Really, most everyone has something in their closet."

"Or on their chest," I added. She made me feel better. Walking into my empty cottage and knowing Beau had gone radio silent made me sad, and I was glad to have a friend ease some of that.

"Red or white?" I asked, holding up two bottles of wine.

"Both," she replied. We started with the red wine.

"The worst part of all this isn't the women in book club. Or Ben. Or even Abby. I'm a big girl. The worst part is that Beau hasn't spoken with me since the fundraiser. No texts. No calls. No visits. It's been almost a week. Total radio silence."

"That does suck." Two bottles of wine later, we still had not resolved that issue.

TWENTY-ONE

MISSY HAD FALLEN asleep on the couch. I left her a blanket and headed to bed. I was unable to sleep. I tossed and turned all night. My head spinning from wine and a barrage of thoughts. No Beau. A book club of angry, divorced women who now really hated me. I couldn't text Emily to tell her the mess I found myself in. I was grateful for Missy. She oddly seemed to understand.

I heard Missy leave early in the morning. Her efforts to keep quiet were appreciated but not enough to keep me from stirring. I incoherently mumbled "goodbye" from my room and rolled back to sleep.

I woke to the smell of coffee and the realization that I had finally fallen asleep hard. I thought maybe it was my internal clock telling me it was time to start the day with the magical elixir of life, even imagining the smell in my sleep. I dragged my heavy head out of bed, rubbing my eyes as I walked towards the kitchen. I really did smell coffee.

"I thought you left earlier," I said as I walked into the kitchen, thinking Missy must have returned. I looked up to see Beau holding a cup of coffee towards me. I stopped in my tracks. I didn't know if I should be angry or happy. I took the coffee without saying anything. I inhaled deeply, letting the smell awaken my senses and help me find balance. He still had not spoken, watching me, waiting.

I sipped my coffee, still unsure what I wanted to say. Or if I should be the one saying anything at all. I couldn't read him. That moment reminded me that I didn't really know this man. Was I naive to think we could fall in love with each other so quickly and believe there wouldn't be drama? Who could have predicted *that* drama? What I did expect from Beau, the man I had fallen in love with for his honesty and candor, was communication. I did not think he would run and hide, too afraid to confront a complicated, uneasy situation.

"It's been a week," I finally said.

"Six days. I know." He still didn't move, frozen in his space.

"That was cruel."

"I know. I'm sorry. I..."

"No. I've been crushed. You have no idea what this week has been like for me. You were the one person I thought would..." I couldn't finish that thought. Midway through, I realized the average person couldn't understand it. "Why wouldn't you stop and talk to me? Or, at least in the past week, reach out to me. I expected so much more."

"I've always been good at fucking up expectations." I took a breath, wanting to tell him that expectation wasn't the right word. He had given me the impression that we wouldn't hide our feelings, knowing the darkness we both experienced in our marriages.

"Honesty, Beau. Not running away," I finally said.

"It was a lot to process. I didn't want to blow up there. I was pissed at Abby for trying to get in the way. So I went to Ben. And I asked him. And he told me. And it's kind of shitty. Hard to process. Even a little comical. But he's not malicious. And I know once I came into your world, it didn't matter. I wish you would have said something about him."

"It's kind of embarrassing."

"Why? You're beautiful. And desirable."

"I think only men are allowed to be proud of being with women much younger than they are. To be fair, I had no idea how old he was. Anyway, it is embarrassing, and it's done. We didn't say anything because we both love you."

He stepped towards me and wrapped his arms around me, pulling me into an embrace. "I missed this," he said. I pulled away from him and looked him in the eyes. I was searching.

"So why stay away? You didn't answer my texts or calls or make any effort to let me know we were okay or even that you were okay."

"I wasn't mad at you. I was mad at her. She's always stirring the pot. Making shit up."

"Except she didn't."

"Total transparency?"

"Please."

"She was right. I really hate that part. I just know that I love you so much. And it's fast. But at this age, we don't have time to waste. And I was just trying to put all the pieces together. And I got in my own way. But I didn't want to get in both our ways. So, I'm rambling." I kissed him to finally shut him up.

"It would have been nice to get proof of life."

"But I did leave you proof of life," he said, confusing me.

"You didn't notice the rocks out on your deck?" I walked to the back of the house. At first, I did not see anything. But in the far corner of the deck was a small rock sculpture with six rocks stacked on each other. He put his arms around my waist from behind, nuzzling my neck.

"A rock a day while I was away."

"That's sweet. I didn't notice. But I've been distracted."

"I was always close. I just needed to filter my brain."

I turned to face him. "So, I've been branded a home wrecker, adulterer, whore, harlot, bitch. The list goes on." He looked at me, puzzled. "Abby told book club."

His reaction was not anger. He was not mortified. "Of course, she did. And now we can move on. And she can stew in her own shit."

"She's got a pretty solid posse. I'm not sure I can ever go back."

"Scar, don't let her do that. Those women will forget soon enough."

"And if they can't?"

"Then they weren't worth it in the first place. Start your own book club. You can call it Scarlet's Harlots." He laughed at his own joke.

"Haha. I already am a scarlet letter." He thought about that.

"Yes. The Scarlet...?" Thankfully, he understood the reference to Nathaniel Hawthorne's "The Scarlet Letter."

"I'm going with D. Divorcee. Seems to be the most all-encompassing."

"If that's the label they give you, it's only because they can see themselves in you. Because, hello, it's a divorced women's book club. Right? I mean, that's the kettle calling the pot black if there is ever a better example."

He was right. If I wanted to feel like this was home, I would have to own my part. I couldn't erase what had happened. I knew people would be silently cheering me on and others vociferously expressing disdain for the immoral intruder. As long as I had Beau and Missy, I would be okay.

We walked back inside. I needed more coffee. The last few moments of revelation had been a lot on minimal caffeine. I walked to the Nespresso machine. I waited as the coffee slowly filled the cup. I took a deep breath, taking in the aroma and feeling a sense of calm. The storm of uneasiness had subsided. I had hoped Beau was above the drama and would only need time; I was right.

When I turned around armed with coffee, Beau sat at the counter, smirking. He was holding a guitar on his lap.

"So, I admit that part of why I needed an extra day was because I wanted this to be perfect."

"What's this?" I asked as I sat on the stool directly across from him, our knees brushing.

"It's your song."

"You wrote me a song?" I was floored.

"Sort of. It's your song. The poem you had on the counter last week. I took a picture of it. I thought I'd try to put those words to music. I tinkered with it a little. It's rough. I wanted to surprise you."

I was speechless. I could tell he was nervous. He was rambling. I wanted to smile as I watched him wrestle with the words. I had never seen him uncomfortable in sharing his emotions with me. I stayed stoic. Maybe I wanted to see him squirm just a little.

"I wanted it to be perfect. But I knew it would never be, and it was just me being a little scared you might not want me back."

"I have no doubt you did my words justice," I said.

"And I think it should be a duet."

"I don't sing," I jumped in.

"I thought the part where she questioned things needed a second voice telling her to stop, telling her he's there, that it'll be alright." He kissed me tenderly. "You are taking me back, right?"

"I never let you go," I said. "I just wish you wouldn't have made me wait so long. I really missed you."

He positioned the guitar in his lap, scooting back from me just enough to comfortably play. He took the song out of his back pocket, unfolded it, and placed it on the counter, smoothing it out so he could read it. He wiped his hands, the left one first, then his right. He gently cleared his throat. "Geez, I'm nervous."

"Me too," I said. I was. I had never had my words turned into a song before. Even if he changed everything, the idea he found something I wrote meaningful enough to put to music was scary.

"Obviously, first draft. Just acoustic. I'm not great," he was stalling.

"It'll be perfect. Please play it."

He looked at his paper and began strumming a chord on his guitar. He stopped once to tighten a string, then started over. He looked at me, smiled, then began:

Do you think about me?
Wonder what I'm doing?
Where I might be?
Have a sentimental thought?
A trigger memory?
Chorus:
I wish I could say
You didn't invade my thoughts
A hundred times a day
Or that you don't come at me in the middle of the night
Fill my mind with desire

Burning a hole right through my heart
I break a little every day
Shattered pieces of my heart hiding on full display
I woke up in the morning
Found myself gasping for air
My heart was racing
Was it feelings of despair?
I opened my eyes and found you there
Me wearing your T-shirt
My hair a mangled mess
But when I saw you
A calm came over me
Were you the answer to my happily?
Or were you a darkness I didn't want to let in?
Chorus:
I wish I could say
You didn't invade my thoughts
A hundred times a day
Or that you don't come at me in the middle of the night
Fill my mind with desire
Burning a hole right through my heart
I break a little every day
Shattered pieces of my heart hiding on full display
My head is spinning
I am so confused by you
If I let you in, will you run and go?
Am I too dangerous?
Will I error again?
What if I hurt you

Like I did him?

He stopped singing for a moment. Without looking up from the paper, he said, "So this is the part I thought would be the duet, the male voice, or female. I guess it doesn't matter. But I thought it should be the last word kind of thing." He repeated the chorus, strummed an extra chord, then sang the final verse.

Duet Voice:
If it's wrong to love again,
Then let's never be right
I will sweep your broken pieces
Repair them with my love
Put you back together again
And fill the empty spaces
We will be each other's glue
Shattered pieces together until we're through.

He finished and looked up from the paper. By then, I was in tears, wiping my snotty nose on my sleeve. I couldn't speak.

"I called it "Shattered Pieces." You didn't have a name for your poem. But it seemed to fit." He put his guitar down. He rubbed my leg with one hand and held my not-snotty hand with his.

"It's so beautiful. The ending. Wow!" I said, trying not to sob.

"I wanted it to reflect us. You're my Scarlet."

"God, I love you." With all my heart, I did. At that moment, I felt all the pain of the last week released from my body. I had been tense, uptight, and in knots for the better part of a week, wondering about this man's love for me. He gently wiped a tear from my eye.

"I love you back," he finally said.

We got up and walked to the bedroom. Our bodies were hungry for each other. We slid under the messy sheets I had just awoken from what seemed hours ago. I had been awake less than an hour. I went to bed sad without Beau. But he had returned to his place in my bed. All felt right in the world again.

We made love and fell asleep until noon. There was something almost surreal about not worrying about time. When in our lives before now had we ever had the time to get to know someone? There was no work, no family obligations, just time together.

Time without boundaries, without an hourglass's regulated measure of time, allowed us to pick the pace. The abruptness of our love and the speed with which it all happened made everything much more intense. It was rapid fire. But it was perfect for us. We weren't on a clock. We were each other's here and now. The intensity was high. The unavoidable drama is even more so. But we could see each other, and I did not want to envision a world without Beau to me. Our time is finite. That was the part that scared me. *Old love is beautiful love*, I thought to myself. "We aren't old," I heard Beau say, realizing I had said it out loud.

"LET'S LIVE TOGETHER," he said after our later-than-usual morning swim. It was out of the blue. "It's silly for you to pay for this place. I have one."

I thought about it, admitting to myself the thought had crossed my mind. And I struggled with it. I liked having my own place – even if it was a rental. I had made it mine. As much as I loved waking up to Beau every morning, the thought of giving up something I had worked to make mine was difficult. It felt selfish on my part. Here was a man who wanted to make life easier for me, for us. But I knew the flipside was going to a place that was his. It was not neutral.

Shane and I bought our first house together. It was ours. Beau and Abby had remodeled his childhood home together. It was theirs. I knew he meant it most genuinely. But there was that part of his home that would always be a part of Abby. Her fingerprints were still there. It didn't matter if he painted the walls differently or bought new furniture. Their home was theirs. For him, it held memories beyond that of his mom and new beginnings here. But when he and Abby were married, they lived there, remodeled, added on, tore down, built up. They had done it all. It was their home. It would be hard for me not to see that, to feel like I was intruding on something they built. And it didn't matter how many times Beau would reassure me.

"Abby wanted the house. Probably because she knew what it meant to me. But I put my foot down. We made it ours, but it was always my mom's first. And thankfully, when my mom passed away, the house was left to me. And I didn't have to share my inheritance. Thank God we never changed the title. Maybe I had a feeling even then." He shrugged his shoulders. "It has always been evolving. It can evolve with you, with us."

The other part was the sense of not having anything to call mine, and I think that was the part I had the hardest time reconciling. My inner voice was telling me that I needed to temper that with the realization that this man was asking me to start a life with him. I would still have what I got from the divorce. I realized I needed to view that as a safety net just in case, but not as the be-all and end-all of my happiness.

"No? Bad idea?" He asked when I didn't reply.

"No. Not a bad idea. I love it." I was less than convincing.

"So, what's bothering you? Too soon?"

"I have a lease." I was stalling.

"Okay, after that."

"I love you. I am so happy with you. But moving to your house with your memories is hard. It's different when you buy something as a couple. It becomes yours together. I miss my house. I miss having something that is mine. It's like losing a part of myself that I just found again."

"That's fair. And I get it." In his usual thoughtful way, he had a solution. "What if we take one of the rooms and make it just yours? The house is big enough. And I will want you to feel like you belong there. Like it's yours, too."

"You'd do that?"

"You're kidding, right? If you asked me, I'd burn the whole thing down so I wouldn't lose you."

"You would not."

"No. But, still. You get it." He pulled me in tight.

"Okay."

"Okay, you'll move in?"

"Yes." He grabbed my face and kissed me hard.

"You make me so happy, Scar." *And, you me, Beau.* I hope my head can stay out of my heart's way.

"Oh, also. What do you think about Calabash?" He said, changing subjects without missing a beat.

"That's random. Is that food?" He laughed.

"Actually, it is too. But it's this beautiful town on the water in North Carolina, barely over the state line. They call themselves the seafood capital of the world. We can just go for the day, have a nice sunset dinner, explore a little. Maybe we can figure out why you think Nicholas Sparks created false expectations. I mean, I am South Carolina, so I'm not rooting for North Carolina."

"I'm pretty convinced South Carolina was a good choice. But I'd love to go to Casablanca with you."

He smiled his big grin. "Calabash."

"There, too," I said with an equally big smile.

TWENTY-TWO

WE SET out for a Saturday in Calabash, driving the two hours north along the coast. I marveled at how green everything was. Tall, beautiful trees lined the highway as we drove. They were full and lush. Beau knew all the different types: Magnolias, Hickory, Sourwood, Dogwood, Elms, and the bright Black Tupelo with its star-shaped leaves. We did not have trees like this along the Southern California coast.

When Henry and Emily were younger, we would take weekend family camping trips to the local mountains at Big Bear. It was nice for the kids to experience that kind of nature away from the palm trees and beaches that they knew on a daily. I remarked to Beau that Northern California was totally different from Southern California in terms of its green landscape and wet weather. He had never been to California before. "Not even to Disneyland?" I asked when he shared that with me.

"Why? We have Disneyworld a quick trip away. And we have beaches, and instead of going to Hawaii, we have way too many options in the Caribbean."

"Yea. Kind of makes you wonder why anyone would come west to visit," I admitted.

"Right? You get it," he said, kind of cocky.

"I'd like to show you my California sometime. We don't have to go to Disneyland. I promise."

"I would love to see your California. Maybe over the holidays. After you've moved in."

I was suddenly struck by the reality of the holidays. What would they look like now that Shane and I weren't together? Where would Henry and Emily go? I know neither of them felt they had a home anymore. "If by home you mean a place to store your extra stuff, then no. But neither of you has lived here full-time since you were eighteen," I reminded them.

I understood that it disrupted their memories of growing up. I was sad, too, to have left my home with my stuff. But it was superficial. The memories had been captured and carefully documented in way too many photo albums. No one, and nothing takes that part away. After reiterating that several times with both, they got it. But holidays—that was an entirely different thing.

"This will be the first year we aren't together for the holidays. There is no home for the kids to come back to," I said.

"That was the hardest part for me. For them. They were about the same age as your kids then. They were doing their own thing. It was base. And I know they felt pulled between me and Abby. I'm sure she didn't make it easy for them to choose to spend time with me. She is a master at pulling the guilt card."

"So, how do you and Abby handle holidays?" I asked.

"It's not as hard to manage when you live in the same town. Ben usually stayed at my house. Bella went with her mom. Now, Bella has her own family, and they usually go to her husband's. He has a big family; his parents are still married. Bella doesn't like drama, and she's incredibly indecisive. Ben was in the military for ten years, making his visits unpredictable and sporadic at best."

Beau reached for my leg, gently rubbing it. "It has a way of working itself out."

I grabbed his hand and held it still in mine. "I know. Still makes me a little sad. And summer's ending means I have to start thinking about this stuff."

He squeezed my leg. "That can wait. We just crossed into North Carolina. Did you feel the Nicholas Sparks magic romance dust fall on you?"

I read the sign welcoming us to North Carolina, which was quickly followed by the Calabash city limits sign.

"It's literally almost South Carolina," I said.

"But it's still North Carolina. If you love it here so much, I'll keep driving you up north...until you don't."

"You are so confident I will not like North Carolina better."

"I am not in North Carolina, so I must be confident."

The GPS took us to the center of town. We parked the car and planned to spend our day walking throughout the town. We grabbed two lattes to-go at a small café and shared a slice of pumpkin bread as we walked. "I love pumpkin bread. I just hate that it's a sign summer is almost over," I said.

"I love it because of that. The trees will change color. Lose their leaves. It cools off. Not so humid."

"I'm excited to experience seasons. Again, something we don't have in Southern California."

"You have not lived until you've experienced seasons." He opined.

"Clearly. I have been under a rock for five and a half decades." He grabbed my hand, interlocking our fingers, and we walked, sipping lattes and taking in the scenic views and serene waters that wove their way throughout the town. I loved this part of the Carolinas. Water was everywhere: the ocean, canals, streams, rivers, ponds, and lakes. Islands and inlets, dog legs and peninsulas. Bridges connecting people to places. None of it ever felt chaotic or contrived. More than anything, I appreciated that things were slower. People were not in a hurry. Nicholas Sparks wrote of North Carolina because he knew the charm of his home state. He could have written about South Carolina. I'm convinced it has the same magic.

Beau knew the requisite spots to visit in Calabash. "Was this a favorite family place? Or somewhere you'd come with Abby?" I had to ask.

"When the kids were young, we'd take weekend trips up and down the coast, visiting the various historical landmarks, stopping to play on the different beaches. Eat glorious seafood. But that stopped before they were teenagers. I started coming back here after the divorce. It was a little piece of paradise far removed from anyone or anything remotely resembling my life. It was meditative, if you want to call it that."

I admit to being relieved to learn it was not a shared recent memory. He had made this his refuge from the bitterness of divorce. He found solace and peace here. It gave him comfort, and he wanted to share that with me.

He took me to the Sunset River Gallery. It was a large, vibrant gallery full of artwork from local artists and even some better-known national artists. The artwork was a rich tapestry of talent. I loved how the gallery showcased local artists, giving them a space to display their works. I became immersed in the beauty around me. What I loved about art was that no two paintings were ever the same. One artist's view of seagulls skimming the ocean waves differed from the next. Nuanced colors, long brushstrokes, or short, sweeping ones. And the way they saw it might be different from how it would be received by the audience.

We spent a significant amount of time there. "Thank you for sharing that with me. I forgot how much I love looking at art, trying to understand it," I said.

"I'm glad. I liked watching you. Pensive. Dreamy. It was fun."

We finished our day in Calabash at the Waterfront Seafood Shack on the water's edge. We watched boats come in with their fresh haul from the day's catch. We dined on succulent shrimp and the renowned Calabash-style fried fish. I tried hush puppies for the first time. And I will spend the rest of my life eating them to make up for all the years I did not know about them. We deviated from our usual wine and enjoyed a cold beer with dinner. It was the perfect ending to the perfect day.

The town had ambiance and radiated positive energy. I could see where it would have helped Beau find his balance again. As we walked the streets of this idyllic southern town, I would occasionally glance at Beau and think I couldn't imagine the rest of my life without him.

We strolled along the water's edge as we walked back to the car. The sun was setting, casting its magnificent orange hues, hanging on to the last light as long as it could before setting beneath the horizon, leaving us with a gentle brush of color. I almost heard it whisper, "I'll be back tomorrow."

Tomorrow is not promised, they say. At this point in my life, I saw that with clarity. It was not lost on me how fortunate I was to be in this moment. With this man. A second chance at life, at love. We're never too old for new beginnings. Tomorrow isn't promised, but it's beautiful to realize the potential for it.

We drove in contented silence out of North Carolina and back towards home. As we crossed the state line back into South Carolina, I turned to Beau and said, "North Carolina's got nothing on you."

Without looking at me, he smiled big and said, "I know."

TWENTY-THREE

THE DAY with Beau gave me a new sense of belonging. Maybe there was something meditative about Calabash. Or, after the chaos of the week prior, I needed a final dose of clarity.

We pulled into the front of my cottage. I loved how quaint it looked outside, even in the dark of night. It felt like home. I liked it here. At that moment, though, I realized that a large part of that feeling came from knowing that Beau was there. In those days when he was gone, it felt empty. He was missing from the everyday part of what made living here so ideal.

"I love this place. It's been perfect. But it was so empty when you were gone. I like having you around," I said as I stared at the porch light flickering.

"If you don't want to live together, I can understand. It's okay," he said as he tucked a strand of hair behind my ear.

I turned to him, "No. That's not it. I think I'm slowly realizing that I want my home to be with you. You are the home. Not the house."

I could hear him exhale a giant breath of relief. "Oh, thank God. But on your timing. I'm good with that."

"Thanks. I do appreciate that. And I have to find someone to take over my lease. In the meantime, let's go inside. I think you should give me one more reminder as to why South Carolina is better than North Carolina. I mean, Calabash was pretty romantic," I teased.

He hastened to open the door, mumbling, "I'm going to give you a list of reasons." He hustled to my side of the door, opened it, grabbed my hand, gently tugging me from the car, pulling me tight in his arms. He kissed me hard. "That's reason number one." I laughed.

"Do I need my pad of paper to take notes?" I asked.

"Nope. My reasons are pretty unforgettable." He turned towards the front of the house, me in tow. It was impossible not to love this man, I thought.

***

"I SWEAR it feels like it's always book club," I told Missy as she sent me a reminder text. That wasn't necessarily true. Time was just flying in my new normal. I was not nearly as busy as I had been in California. But I found a way to become accustomed to a slower pace, enjoying the moments, not rushing from one place to the next so I could cross something off my list. I was learning it wasn't the end of the world if I didn't start something on a particular day or finish it, for that matter. Tomorrow was a new day. And waking up with Beau is a reality of that.

Beau brought me to his house, a beautiful oceanfront property. It was older but nicely renovated. The street was an eclectic mix of homes that had been there forever, and others were spectacular newer mansion-like homes. There had been an infusion of money into the Sullivan's Island real estate market. It was an idyllic place to live. I picked it on a whim. Others picked it with intent. I got lucky. The stars had somehow aligned for me, guiding me to this place, to this man.

He led me to a sunroom at the back of the house. It had large windows that ran the length of the room, and the light was perfect. "This room is beautiful, Beau. What do you use it for?" I asked.

"Reflection," he said, half joking, as the light caught his eye and he had to look away.

"I've never used this room, honestly. And before you ask, Abby never did either. It wasn't big enough to entertain. The kids wanted more privacy. So it's kind of been a nothing room. But, I was thinking..."

"Yes!" I exclaimed before he could finish.

"Yea?"

"This is the most perfect room I've ever seen. The light is spectacular. The view. Stunning."

He pulled out several swatches of paint and handed them to me. "Then it's yours. Make it yours, Scar. I want you to love it." He kissed me. "The room already looks so much more alive with you in it."

"Why, Mr. Sanders, you make me swoon. I do hope you take advantage of me in this room someday."

"Someday?" he asked as he lifted my sundress off me. "Just being in here with you has me excited. See?" I looked down and laughed.

"I like having that effect on you. But does a lady do this kind of stuff?"

"Stuff? You mean have sex in a sunroom with the world just outside?" I nodded. "My lady does."

And just like that we were on the floor in the sunroom, light bouncing off the walls, the world outside oblivious to the two of us finding pleasure in our naked bodies.

We lay on the floor, staring at the large ceiling above us. "I never realized what a cool room this really is," he said.

"It's pretty amazing. Thank you for letting me make it mine."

He got up on his elbow and looked at me. "One stipulation. I cannot promise I will not attempt to distract you when you're hard at work. This light makes you even more beautiful."

"There you go again with that southern charm. I'm not sure how I got so lucky."

"I'm pretty sure we can blame it on Otis," he joked.

As if on cue, Otis bounded into the room, jumping on top of us, licking our faces and scratching our bodies in the most sensitive places. Beau and I laughed so hard that we both started crying. Otis left momentarily, then returned with a ball in his mouth, nudging it between us.

"Awww. He likes you," Beau said as he wiped a tear from under his eye.

"We already knew that," I said.

"But this was the big test. He's pretty protective of me. So, you know, him sharing a ball is a big deal. It could have been a deal breaker."

I patted Otis on the head as I got up and put my dress back on. When I turned around, Otis was sitting at my feet, ball in mouth, ready to play.

"I think the rest of the house tour needs to be after we take him for a walk," I said. And as soon as I said the word walk, Otis was running in circles, beside himself with joy.

We walked along the beach in front of Beau's home, and Otis happily bound up and down the sandy strand, fetching the ball, chasing birds, and greeting strangers.

Why I hadn't wondered about Otis on the nights Beau was with me suddenly made me feel bad. I loved dogs. I missed mine. I would never have left Zero alone all night, every night, like Beau had been doing for me.

"Do you leave Otis here alone nights you're with me?"

"I do." That made me feel horrible. "But," he stopped and pointed to a small granny flat adjacent to his property. "I rent that little house out. He's been here probably thirty or so years. Jesse. I think he might have loved my mom. Or they had a thing. I don't like to think about it. But he does a lot of work on the house. The kids call him uncle. He's kind of like a dad figure. He loves

Otis. Otis loves him. He'd take care of him when I worked nights. It's a perfect arrangement."

I was relieved to learn this. "I look forward to meeting him." I smiled at Beau. "There's still so much to learn about you."

"I'm really pretty simple. But I'll keep it interesting as long as possible."

"I prefer no big surprises. And no drama. I have had enough of that."

I INSISTED I pick Missy up for our book club. She had been coy about where she lived. We either met at restaurants or at my house when we got together. I wondered if she had been misleading me. Maybe she wasn't from a well-established family with a fancy estate. Perhaps she was playing me all along. It didn't matter. I liked her as a person. She has been there for me since the day we met.

She conceded to my insistence I pick her up, ending the text with, "Okay. But don't judge."

When I arrived at her home, I was immediately stunned by its enormity. I walked up to her front door and rang the bell. I peered in through the panels on the side of the giant front entrance as Missy flung open the door.

"Holy shit, girlfriend. Why you been holding out on me?" I said.

"It's a little over the top, I know. It's kind of embarrassing," she said.

"Why? It's stunning. Totally suits you." I walked into the foyer while she grabbed her purse.

"I'll give you a tour another time." I rolled my eyes in doubt. "I promise."

As we walked to my car, I asked why she would be embarrassed. "I know money is this big thing for people. And I'm by no means ungrateful for all this. But I didn't earn it. I got it when my parents died. And then that wasn't without bitterness by other family members. Hello, Margo? It's complicated. And I'll share it all someday."

"Whenever you're ready. I love a good story."

She stopped and looked at me. "Honestly, growing up, it was sometimes hard to know who your real friends were. I withdrew because I constantly felt like people were using me. To get to my dad. To get access to this lifestyle. There's a lot of self-doubt attached to wealth. I never could have been a Hilton. Or a Kardashian. The limelight makes me uncomfortable."

"But at the fundraiser, you were shining so bright."

"As I've gotten older, I've learned to compartmentalize the different versions of me. I've learned to have fun with them, too. It took leaving Cal and having an affair, not in that order, but life. I hate being judged. Then you came along and were willing to be my friend without any of the bullshit attached to it." She swallowed her words.

"Oh, Missy. You sappy girl, you. Now you got me all teary-eyed." I wiped my eyes. "I'm grateful for you too."

She hugged me and then flapped her hands as if that would dry her eyes and stop her tears.

"Let's go face the firing squad at book club. I'm armed and ready," I said. "Metaphorically speaking."

"Of course," she said with a wink as she got in my car.

We entered the library laughing. Despite the debacle of the last book club, I kept an open mind. These women had no more right to judge me than I did to judge them. We all had our stories. None of them were perfect. We were all divorced. We were all trying to navigate middle age and beyond with a D on our chests, whether we were the one scorned or the one scorning.

As I walked in, I tried to remind myself of this. I had been a stranger, open, honest, and overwhelming. That kind of candor was not akin to the proper Southern women they pretended to be. But I was choosing to call this place home, and I was not going to retreat because they were bullying me. Abby would not have that on me. I even wondered if someday she and I might be friends. There was a slight chance of that, but maybe we could be cordial.

Audrey, Abby, and Margo were shocked when I walked in. Dahlia was warm and welcoming. There was something I liked about her. I imagine someday Dahlia will share her divorce story over drinks, and it will be juicy, spicy, and not so nice. I looked forward to that. Missy and I sat down next to her.

Audrey stood at the front of the room in her usual effort to commence book club. She was easily irritated at her inability to call us to order. But as we chatted amongst ourselves, the room suddenly became quiet. Audrey looked confused - and satisfied - that she finally had our attention. But we were not looking at her. She noticed this and turned around to see what we were staring at.

Behind Audrey was a beautiful, statuesque woman. She was stunning with her blonde mane perfectly coifed in beach waves, her skin a summer shade of brown. Her figure said I was a model once but then discovered food: thick in the right places to make her look human. She appeared younger than the rest of us—maybe forty. I was terrible at guessing anymore. Her hazel eyes were expressive, and said *I am sad but not defeated.* I liked her instantly.

I looked to Missy, seeking guidance as to why everyone was so surprised to see her. She leaned in. "That's Amber Harris Montgomery." My eyes said, "And..."

"Her husband owns like three sports teams. More money than you'd know what to do with." Again, I shot her a look. "Or I'd know what to do with," acknowledging her own wealth. "She's probably the closest thing to a celebrity we have here."

"So, are they freaking out because she's a celebrity?" I asked as Missy trained her eyes on Amber.

The silence was awkward and long. No one spoke. Amber walked forward, confident and probably a little confused by the silence. Or maybe she was used to it at this point in her life.

"Hi. I'm Amber. I was told I should check out this book club. This is the divorced one, right?" She looked at Audrey as she asked.

"Of course. Yes. Welcome," Audrey finally said as she motioned to an empty chair. Amber stepped towards the chair, surveyed the room, stopped, and spoke. "I need women, friends who understand." I wanted to snicker out loud. Missy held hers in, too. This looked serious.

"Who is Scarlet?" she continued. All eyes turned to me. I slowly raised my hand.

Her demeanor suddenly changed. She relaxed. "Oh my God. I have been dying to meet you. My friends. Anyhow, it doesn't matter. They said you are strong and resilient. And I should make friends with you because you won't judge me. And you'd understand that women aren't always the ones scorned." She spoke directly to me as if we were the only two people in the room. She didn't care about the other women. I was stunned. And suddenly felt like one of the popular girls. Younger women were talking about me. In a good way. The fleeting thought that it might have been Ben entered my mind. Had he said things to preserve my image? I couldn't imagine him ever divulging what happened between us. Maybe he just said I was cool. Whatever it was, the other women in the group were suddenly looking at me differently, like I might have something to offer now. *The irony*, I thought.

I smiled at Amber. Missy grinned ear to ear next to me. We both scooted for Amber to sit next to us. I looked around the room, "We don't bite, I promise." I winked at Abby as I said it.

Unlike me at my first book club, Amber stayed quiet. I could tell she was assessing the women and what she'd just gotten herself into. The women were on their best behavior, staying on topic. They were starstruck by Amber's presence.

I later learned from Missy that Amber came from a modest family on Sullivan's Island. She had been a star volleyball player at Nebraska, did some sports modeling, and then went on the reality show *The Bachelor*. While she didn't get the final rose or meet Mitchell Montgomery on the show, she was afforded a celebrity lifestyle that opened the door to meet him. It was a whirlwind romance. Their relationship and marriage became the fodder of gossip rags.

I could see the women nattering in their group chat or afternoon coffee klatsch, the ones Missy and I would not be part of. I wondered if they would pity her because of her status or condemn her because of her story. They will judge, no doubt. If she sought me out, she would likely know I am not a woman scorned.

Amber survived her first book club. And, for the first time, I did, too. I tempered my comments, agreeing on occasion. I was behaving. I didn't care much about the book whose title I kept forgetting. Audrey's plan to have us read books without controversy proved a good strategy. It was boring, but I welcomed it, given how I started with these women.

Amber walked out with me and Missy after the book club ended.

"What did you think?" I asked as we stood together in front of the library. The other women had quickly disappeared down the street towards Poe's. Even Audrey had managed to leave with them. I could only imagine their haste to start gossiping about Amber Harris Montgomery.

"Honestly, I'm just happy to have a place to go where people aren't judging me," she said in a vulnerable tone.

"Oh, honey, just you wait," Missy said.

"Yeah, these women are pretty brutal. They were really harsh with me. But I'm still here," I said. "I'm curious, though, how'd you know about me?"

"Janice. Well, really, Dahlia. Janice is like a little sister." I knew I liked Dahlia. "I needed to come back here. Away from all the shit. Away from Mitchell. Away from..." she paused. "I cheated on Mitchell. And he found out online. It was horrible. And I felt bad. He wasn't a bad person. He just was never available. I loved him. I still do." She began to tear up.

"It's okay," I said. "My ex wasn't horrible either. Just unavailable. And I cheated. Well, I had an emotional affair. He thought that was worse. So I get it."

Missy added her story, "Total cheater right here, too."

"Do you know how good it feels to tell someone that knowing I'm not going to be judged? So good. Thank you." She threw her arms around us both.

"Are you moving back then? I mean, you did come to our book club," Missy asked.

"For a while. While I figure the next steps out. I'm embarrassed to say I'm living with my parents. Janice is helping me look for a place. It's not easy." I looked at Missy. She looked at me.

"I've got the perfect place for you," I said.

I was happy inside. And I felt happy outside. I was wearing a smile of contented satisfaction.

"I was thinking of starting a new, less discriminatory, decidedly more flawed book club. I want to call it Scarlet's Harlots. You both in?" I asked Missy and Amber as we walked down the street toward Poe's. They both giggled their approval.

TWENTY-FOUR

IT WAS A BEAUTIFUL SUMMER. I had made the right decision to move to Sullivan's Island. My life had become a different version of itself in a few short months. I was living life on my terms. I opened my heart and discovered love with a man who was unexpected. I had made a friend. And I was confident, despite some awkward moments in between, that I would continue to forge friendships inside my divorced women's book club. The letters I brandished on my chest are sometimes still on display, but maybe a lower-case version of themselves instead of the bold capital letters they had been when I first came to town.

I moved in with Beau at the end of the summer. It was fast, we knew. But we also recognized that we were on the back slope of life – even if we were healthy. Our time together was finite. We knew the end was there. We might have twenty years and change. We might not. Life was always unpredictable, but decidedly more so as we got older. It sometimes made me sad to think it took me this long to be good with myself, to accept that I could be loved and love someone. We were unapologetically ourselves. And that was the beauty of our love.

Nicholas Sparks no longer haunts my images of love. North Carolina and its promises of happily ever after felt a million miles away even though, if I squinted hard enough, I might be able to make it out somewhere in the distance.

South Carolina had won my heart. It felt like home here. I began this new life with trepidation about moving across the country to a place I had only visited in small increments, experienced in carefully planned doses. I didn't know if this California girl would feel comfortable. I didn't embrace the label, but I knew it applied. I wanted and needed a new beginning far removed from where I had spent my entire life. Finding my happiness here was not a given. Discovering Beau was unexpected.

We weren't supposed to fall in love. *All the good ones were taken*, they said. But we were the good ones. A little broken in places, maybe. But we were good. And we became even better together. All our broken, missing pieces meshed perfectly like it was what we'd been waiting for our whole lives. Every experience, both good and hard, brought us to each other. How lucky were we to know love at our age? To finally be with the one who filled us with life, laughter, and a love that only a lifetime of experiences would allow? It was not lost on me. It was unexpected. Yes. And it was beautiful. Undoubtedly.

Love at any age isn't promised. You realize that along the way. Maybe it's why we sometimes acquiesce to being okay with the status quo in volatile relationships. Older love and the realization that a lifetime of loving each other truly becomes a matter of twenty or thirty years. But twenty or thirty years of looking someone in the eyes who sees you, every part of you, becomes a satisfying, consoling thought.

Beau and I came to the party imperfectly. We found each other in all our broken pieces and found a way to put them back together again. Sometimes, the edges had to be forced to fit. We found a way to finagle the straight sides to fit the round hole. It wasn't smooth, but it was real. Our imperfections were perfect in the end. The realization understood that we were who we were because of life's experiences. It was working for us at this time in our lives.

No one tells you the beautiful parts of discovering love when you least expect to find it. Certainly, not in the back half of your life when you feel closer to the end than the beginning or even the middle. They don't tell you the benefits of experience. The wisdom of disappointment, the beauty of being unapologetically you.

"I'm just me," Beau would say with a smirk when I said I loved all the parts of him.

"And I am me," I would say, knowing I had come to accept this version: the less-than-perfect woman with the scarlet letter D proudly displayed on her chest as a message of hope, courage, strength, and conviction.

Maybe it's the one we don't see coming. The one we least expected. That fills the parts that weren't whole. We were us. Together. As individuals. All the parts and pieces that made us complete. We knew that. We lived that. We were that.

———

BEAU WALKED UP beside me as I sat mesmerized by the brilliant sunset. I never imagined a world of a waking rising sun in its glorious hues of orange and a setting one equally on fire, seemingly not at all exhausted from the day. He gently kissed my neck and handed me a glass of chardonnay before sitting beside me.

"Hey, beautiful," he said. I believed those words to be true when he spoke them.

"Hi, handsome."

"How lucky are we to have this?" He took my hand, brushing his lips gently against the top as he held it.

"Incredibly."

I raised my glass toward the setting sun and watched as the colors changed with the light, dancing as they reflected off the inside of my glass. I wondered at how my life had changed in a plethora of ways in the last year. But mostly, I marveled at how I almost let Nicholas Sparks interfere.

THE END

ABOUT THE AUTHOR

Kirsten Pursell is a best selling and award winning indie author known for engaging narratives that often blend romance with deeper emotional themes. *Finding Scarlet* was originally released in November 2024 as *The Scarlet D*. It is her fifth novel. Her fourth book, *Long Enough to Love You*, earned numerous awards in women's fiction, divorce fiction and romance and has been an Amazon best seller. Previous works include her memoir, *On Becoming Me: Memoir of an 80's Teenager*, and two additional novels: *Harvard* and *Company Clown*. She lives in Southern California.

ALSO BY KIRSTEN PURSELL

Long Enough to Love You
On Becoming Me: Memoir of an 80's Teenager
Harvard
Company Clown: The rise and fall of a corporate icon